Soot and Slipper

Other Works by Kate Stradling

The *Annals of Altair* Series
A Boy Called Hawk
A Rumor of Real Irish Tea

The *Ruses* Series
Kingdom of Ruses
Tournament of Ruses

Goldmayne: A Fairy Tale

The Legendary Inge

Namesake

Brine and Bone

Soot and Slipper

a novella

Based on Charles Perrault's
"Cinderella, or The Little Glass Slipper"

Kate Stradling

Eulalia Skye Press
MESA, ARIZONA

Soot and Slipper

Copyright © 2019 by Kate Stradling
katestradling.com

All rights reserved. No part of this book may be reproduced or transmitted in any form or by any means, electronic or mechanical, including photocopying, recording, or by any information storage and retrieval system, without written consent of the author.

Published by
Eulalia Skye Press
P.O. Box 2203, Mesa, AZ 85214
eulaliaskye.com

ISBN: 978-1-947495-04-3
Library of Congress Control Number: 2019903235

for my nieces
may you cultivate kindness
and reap the rewards

Preface

DOES THE WORLD need another Cinderella retelling? In a nutshell, no. But sometimes we do things because they're fun, not because they're necessary.

Six months ago, I'd have laughed if someone suggested I write an adaptation of this particular tale. With countless variations of it already in print and film, I didn't see a gap that would require my creative fingerprint to fill. Then five months ago, I stumbled across an angle that intrigued. The more I explored the idea, the more it captivated me. At the time, I needed something light and fluffy and whimsical to write. This pet project, as it were, fulfilled that need admirably.

Cinderella is the brain candy of literature. Everyone knows the set-up and the basic plot progression. We come to any retelling with predefined expectations, and how far the story strays from its original pattern—or from our original perception of it—depends largely on the genre and setting in which its new form occurs.

I chose the traditional route. Charles Perrault's telling provides the base of this novella, although my narrator does a couple of literary hat tips to the Brothers Grimm (if you can find them). My heroine is optimism personified. Her circumstances are roughly what you would expect... and roughly not. The variations arose from questions that the original tale left me unanswered.

In paying homage to my primary source, I drew upon French influences for atmosphere, with a smattering of Italian, Celtic, and Greek added to the mix. Nevertheless, this is a fantasy world. Although it may reflect familiar patterns, it also runs according to its own rules.

Many thanks to my critique partners, Jill Burgoyne and Rachel Collett, who countenanced this fanciful detour from the novel I was *supposed* to be working on; to my mom, Edith, who egged me on after I let her read the first ten pages; to my ANWA chapter-mates who provided excellent feedback on a pivotal scene; and to God, who showed me how to love writing again.

Even literary fluff can be instructive.

So here's my take on the well-known theme of ashes and an infamous glass shoe. I hope you enjoy reading it even half as much as I enjoyed writing it.

K.S.
March 2019

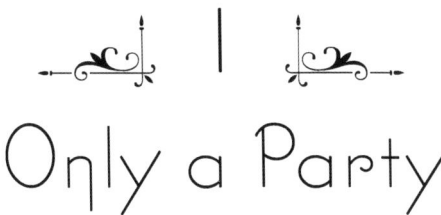

Only a Party

EUGENIE ONLY WANTED to go to a party.

It didn't seem like a lot to ask, but the dying light in her stepmother's eyes said otherwise. Marielle blinked, a rapid reaction to mask her welling tears. When she looked away to the wall with her bottom lip caught between her teeth, Eugenie knew it was too much.

She should have squelched the desire.

"I suppose," Marielle started after a weighty swallow, but her throat choked on anything further. Eugenie crushed her worn apron in clenched fingers, the magnitude of her frivolity striking her in full. In reaction to her dismay, Marielle grasped her wrist with one small hand.

She ducked her head into Eugenie's view—not a difficult task, given her petite stature. "It's not that I don't *want* you to go. It's just—"

"The money," Eugenie finished for her.

Marielle's brows arched, and her feathery voice vaulted into childlike pitches. "No! That is, yes, but not how you think. It's just... this is their chance, Florelle and Aurielle, their chance to mingle with their peers without any stigma of poverty clinging to them. It's not that I don't want you to go, but you're so beautiful, and they're ..."

Not.

She didn't say the word, and guilt flashed across her face, that she could speak of her own children so unfavorably. But she was right. Florelle and Aurielle didn't take after their delicate mother in anything more than stature. They inherited much clumsier features from their father, the late Baron Lavande. His portrait hung in the family gallery—not in a place of prominence, as that would be inappropriate—and every time Eugenie gazed upon the hooked nose she could see Florelle, and the deep-set eyes were Aurielle's own. Their mouths, wide and thin-lipped, bore no resemblance to the puckered rosebud before her now, and their hair hung limp in shades of mouse-brown instead of their mother's lustrous silver-blonde.

It wasn't the younger Elles' fault that they inherited such strong features. Still in the bloom of youth, they were pretty in their own ways, just not according to current social preferences. A masquerade would conceal those surface flaws and allow others to see them as they truly were.

Which wasn't ... great, but at least they wouldn't have any aesthetic judgements working against them.

"Don't you see, Eugenie?" her stepmother asked, her voice warbling as she teetered close to tears. "Once you reach your majority, everything here is completely yours alone. You can cast us all out on the streets if you wish—"

"I would never—!"

She silenced the girl's protest with a forbearing smile. "Of course you say that now, but things change. If you marry, you would want to live here with your husband, and he might not like three extra women underfoot. My daughters and I have nothing to call our own, nothing beyond the small allowance their father left for them, which is hardly enough to live on, as you know."

Eugenie swallowed the rising lump in her throat. A fortune awaited her, a fortune that her stepmother refused to touch. Her stepsisters had gone to finishing school on the remnants of their father's wasted estates, pinning their matrimonial hopes on acquiring as much gentility as they could. They returned with social graces and affectations, eager to please any prospective husband with their twittering laughs and fluttering lashes.

Marielle's smile faded as her eyes became distant. "If either one of them can find a husband thanks to these masquerades, all our futures will be secure. As long as ... don't take this the wrong way, Eugenie. As long as the gentleman doesn't develop a preference for you instead."

Eugenie blushed to the roots of her golden hair, her face afire. Any man who would transfer his affections based on looks wasn't worth having. And if he transferred them after already engaging himself to another, doubly so.

Her disappointment retreated behind a mask of false good cheer. "I don't have to go. It was only a whim. Of course I'll stay home."

Her stepmother tempered her relief with regret. "I'm so sorry. We'll make it up to you, somehow." And she squeezed Eugenie's hand in reassurance before releasing her again. Her attention shifted to the piles of yellow satin and iridescent gauze upon the work table. "The costumes are coming along beautifully."

Eugenie's nerves bubbled up her throat in an anemic chuckle. "I'm only working with your old dresses. Sun, moon, and stars. If you're not careful, you might steal away their suitors yourself."

Marielle's laugh tinkled like a small, silver bell. "As long as he's rich, it doesn't matter."

The words twisted her stepdaughter's heart. That a lady of title and refinement should be reduced to such mercenary ambitions—

But such it was. Marielle had neither skill nor stamina to earn her own living and remained at the mercy of social standards she didn't create.

And the best Eugenie could do was support her.

So she would continue to sew and alter and embroider, and when the grand evening arrived, she would stay home.

Even though she wanted more than anything in the world to go.

2
Mischief Sparked

THE CARRIAGE RATTLED past the manor gates, teetering as it settled into the worn wheel tracks on the main road. Within, three elegantly dressed silhouettes leaned close, chattering their excitement to one another. The piercing sun, low in the sky, illuminated them through the back window.

They didn't even glance behind them. The carriage passed beyond sight, and Eugenie's shoulders drooped on a sigh.

Why did she always linger to watch them leave? They never turned to wave that one last farewell. She hugged her arms close, staving off the inevitable disappointment.

Her father used to wave half a dozen times between the house and the posts that marked the estate boundaries. He would pause to blow kisses and shout for her to behave.

A piece of her heart had died with him four years ago. It wasn't the Elles' responsibility to revive it, yet still she waited on the manor steps every single time they left.

In resignation, she turned her back on the sunset and trudged to the garden, weary to her very bones. The past five days had been nothing but sewing, from early in the morning to late at night. The Elles had even taken over kitchen duties so she could stay on task—a mixed blessing, as none of them could cook.

She should make herself a proper meal tonight, but it wasn't worth the effort. They would eat at the masquerade, and she could make do with whatever scraps she could glean from the kitchen. Despondency had withered her appetite anyway.

With another sigh she plopped onto a stone bench and lay flat, its residual summer warmth pressing through the back of her worn cotton dress.

"It's no use getting depressed, Eugenie," she said aloud, staring up at the slate-colored clouds against the orange sky. "You couldn't have made another costume even if Marielle had said you could go."

Her fingertips ached in response, raw from all the beading and stitching she had accomplished in such a short time. The other noble houses would have hired seamstresses, but the House of Pluterra had no such funds to spare. Eugenie, the only one with any practical sewing skills, had been making their clothes ever since her stepmother discovered that she liked such needlework. What had started as a mere hobby while she recovered from an extended illness became almost an occupation.

But it was fine. The Elles had their fashionable clothes, and Eugenie avoided any guilt that her father had left the whole of his estate to her and only a small remembrance to each of them.

Even so, three full costumes in only five days was really too much. The palace should have given more notice that they were reviving the old tradition of weekend masquerades.

She shut her eyes as the vermillion sky transitioned to indigo darkness. If the Elles wanted to attend more than one masquerade, she needed to start a new set of costumes now. They were the sun, moon, and stars tonight—Solella, Lunella, and Astrella, she had gleefully announced as she presented them with the finished ensembles.

Florelle had pounced on the golden, frothy confection with its sparkling mask, and Aurielle snatched up the silver one. Their mother, with a faint smile at her lips, accepted the dark, spangled dress her daughters had bypassed. Everything went exactly as Eugenie had predicted. Her stepsisters preferred flashy colors, but the starry dress was the prettiest of the group.

Much like Marielle.

"There wasn't room for another costume in that set anyway," she said aloud.

"Wasn't there?" a pleasant voice replied.

Her eyes flew open. She sat up, but the garden around her remained silent and empty. A chill swept down her spine in spite of the late summer warmth.

Had she imagined those words? Was her soul-gnawing loneliness finally getting to her? Ridiculous. She wouldn't wallow in self-pity.

"There wasn't," she said firmly.

The disembodied voice echoed around her, its ethereal harmonics thrumming through her ribcage. "Perhaps you're right. But I don't see why you should have to match their set anyway."

Great. She really was cracking.

But, if that was the case, why not embrace it?

"I don't *have* to match their set, but when I don't try, it's like I'm rejecting them."

"But you can't match them, and you know it."

Something flickered across her vision, in that jittering sensation that often happened when she had gone too many hours without sleep. The estate lay too near the forest for such nighttime hallucinations not to terrify. She hefted from the bench, intent upon seeking out her bed in the east wing of the manor house.

"You want to go, don't you? To the masquerade? I wouldn't be here if you didn't."

Her footsteps halted, crushing the fragrant summer grass beneath her. All around her, the sounds of twilight flurried: insects buzzing and frogs croaking in the nearby pond. Her skin crawled with apprehension. She shouldn't engage with disembodied voices. The forest teemed with wood sprites and sylphs, creatures she had glimpsed as a child.

Age always dimmed such fanciful sight. She hadn't thought of them in years.

"I can't go," she said, staring at the dull, worn toes of her shoes. "I don't have a costume, and I don't have a way there, and I'm too tired tonight anyway." But a smothered hope whirled from the depths of her soul. She slid her gaze upward, to where the first stars patterned the darkening sky.

What would it be like, to enter the glittering crowds of nobility, to dance among them, to feel their music and energy thrum through her for one glorious night? She was a starving beggar learning of a banquet she could not attend, yet even the chance to press her nose against the window quickened her heart.

"Those are excuses, not obstacles," said the disembodied voice.

"Who are you?" Eugenie asked, looking around herself in earnest now.

A ghostly figure shimmered on the breeze, the flash of a firefly at its heart. Her pulse jumped. Had she accidentally crossed a fairy circle in her listlessness? Fairies were dangerous.

"I'm your godmother, child," said the voice, confirming her worst fears.

Soot and Slipper

"I don't have a godmother." Eugenie edged toward the house, ready to break into a run. She would go inside, lock the door, and curl up by the fire with a thick blanket and her sketchbook. In the morning, this would be nothing more than the last vestiges of a strange dream.

But even as she shifted her weight to bolt, the ghostly glimmer solidified with a pop.

"Oh, play along, would you?" said the fairy. The sheer consternation on her face evoked an instinctive laugh. Eugenie bit her lips to control the irrational mirth, her eyes huge. With such a physical manifestation before her, she dared not escape.

Hair the color of flames curled upward in an impossible pile atop a head that was *slightly* too big for its elegant body. Fairies couldn't produce a perfect human likeness, but this one had done a decent job. The vibrant folds of lace and gauze that encased her spindly limbs might have doubled as a masquerade costume. Eugenie mentally catalogued its construct for later contemplation.

Her lack of movement encouraged the fairy. "You will play with me, won't you?" the creature asked, suddenly hopeful.

Eugenie mutely shook her head.

The delicate expression flattened. "You can play with me, or I can play with you. Which would you prefer?"

Fairy threats were no laughing matter, but hearing one from such a childlike figure struck her sense of the ridiculous. "Is there a difference?" she asked. "It'll cause mischief either way."

"In the first I cause mischief *with* you, and in the second I cause it *against* you," said her supernatural visitor. But any sternness melted away in a pleading, percussive stamping of her feet. "Oh, do play along. I'm so *bored*! Why can't you let me send you to a party you want to go to anyway?"

It seemed like a simple enough request, but dealings with fairies rarely were.

"What do you get in return?" Eugenie asked.

"Nothing. Satisfaction for a job well done. Mischief accomplished."

She was lying, of course. Fairies always lied. "I'm not signing any contracts," Eugenie said.

"Nobody asked you to," the creature sniped. "Just let me dress you up and send you on your way."

"That's it? How does that make any mischief at all?"

Starlight twinkled in the too-large eyes, and a pair of dimples popped to her cheeks. "It'll make more than you know."

"Then I'd better not," said Eugenie, dragging her toe through the ragged grass. A low rumble from the fairy made her watchful. She peered upward through long lashes, tense as she awaited some dreadful spell.

Instead, the creature stamped her foot again. "Oh, let me do it! If you're back before midnight, you won't suffer any ill effects, and you're tired anyway, so why should you stay longer than that?"

"Why should I go at all?" Eugenie asked.

The pointed face thrust near her, the otherworldly eyes glimmering. "Because you *want* to. Because you're slowly dying here and you don't even know it. Because there's a whole sparkling world beyond this nook where you live, and your heart yearns to explore it but you chain your body here out of a duty you don't owe and that no one will ever repay you."

The words washed through her, keen and cutting. She swallowed against rising emotions, blinking rapidly.

A dream. This was only a dream. In the morning, she would look back at it and laugh.

Soot and Slipper

The fairy grinned on a grunt. "I'm right, aren't I? I've watched you long enough. I know what lies in your heart. Let me *help* you."

Eugenie abandoned any pretense of coyness. "If I let you 'help' me, I get punished for it later to restore the balance. I know how fairy magic works."

A beleaguered sigh wrenched from the creature's throat, her expression contorted. She spun on one dainty foot and paced to the stone bench, then back again. "Fine. You're not the one I'm helping. You're the punishment I'm using to restore balance. Are you happy now? Keep to the boundaries I set, and you won't fall into any fairy consequences."

"Who are you punishing?" Eugenie asked in concern. "I can't help you do that. And even if I were the punishment, doesn't your act of helping me only start the cycle over again?"

"So many questions," the fairy muttered, kicking the ground. "I thought you'd leap at the chance, but no." Her gaze hardened. "Eugenie Vivienne, I *can't* punish you. You've already been punished and you don't even know it. And if the world stays out of balance much longer, *I'm* the one who gets to suffer for it."

It was all tosh, a fairy using every persuasion she could to get her way. Still, the chill in Eugenie's spine redoubled. She shook her head to clear away the compulsive words.

A wheedling plea emerged next. "It's only a *party*, three or four hours at most by the time you get there."

That was true enough. Plus, the fairy knew her name. If she wanted to cast mischief against her, she could.

And, after all, Eugenie did want to go to the masquerade.

"But I don't have a costume," she said.

The dimples returned in full force. "That is easily done. A costume and carriage, in return for your promise to be home before the clock strikes twelve. Do we have a deal? Not a deal," she corrected before Eugenie could protest. She pinched the bridge of her sharp nose with delicate fingers. "Do you understand the boundaries?"

This was a terrible idea. Or a brilliant one. Eugenie wasn't quite sure which. "What happens if I don't come home in time?"

"Your costume and carriage melt into fairy dust and you have to walk all the way back."

That didn't sound so bad—if the fairy was telling the truth.

But she seemed sincere, and the longer they bartered, the less time Eugenie would have to enjoy the spectacle of a royal masquerade. Perhaps if she'd had more sleep she would have resisted more staunchly.

"All right, then. I'll go."

Surprise—joy, anticipation, giddy elation—leapt to the creature's face. She squealed and clapped her hands. "I knew you would! You won't regret it, I promise!"

Eugenie squelched her instinctive misgivings and maintained a note of disinterest in her voice. "What sort of costume are you sending me in?"

The fairy blew a hanging strand of red hair out of her face, arms crossed and gaze scrutinizing. "You can't match the frivolous set who just left. I'll make you their opposite instead."

The opposite of the sun, moon, and stars? "What could that possibly be?" Eugenie asked.

Her fairy godmother danced a circle around her, mischief emanating from her like warmth from a fire. "You, my lovely child, are going as soot."

3
Masquerade

NEVER HAD SOOT felt so glamorous.

Eugenie rubbed her fingers against one another, relishing the soft black satin of her evening gloves. Her coal-dark dress fit close in the bodice and billowed out in a smoky skirt, glittering with chips of jet and polished onyx. The slippers, cut from obsidian, cushioned her feet as though made of kid instead, and the velvet half-mask framed her eyes and covered her nose as though molded there. Her blonde hair, gathered in ringlets that dangled from one side of her head, spoiled the effect of soot and smoke, but her fairy benefactress had refused to do anything about the color.

"I'm not *ruining* that shade of gold, not even for a few hours. You're only *playing* cinder-soot, not taking it as your new identity."

The carriage was a misty contraption formed from shadows and crawling vines. The horses, conjured from pond frogs, kept a quick, steady pace through the darkened countryside from her father's estate to the palace on the outskirts of Jacondria's capital city. The ride passed like a dream, as though wings carried her.

Perhaps they did. She arrived faster than any mortal horses could run. When the coach stopped in the courtyard and the door opened, she stepped to paved stones and looked up in wonder.

Light suffused the regal building. Music floated on the night breeze, and her heart soared with it. Had she been exhausted an hour ago? It seemed like another lifetime.

Perhaps she was dreaming after all.

She picked up her skirts and climbed marble stairs to the entrance, where guards and servants mingled. They parted to let her pass, inclining their heads in respect.

She fought her rising self-consciousness. A true lady should always arrive with a chaperone, and she had none. But the royal masquerades were open to any who wished to attend, peasant or noble, as long as they wore a costume and a mask.

Past the first line of servants, the great hall opened before her. Stairs descended to a white marble floor where vibrant guests danced and flirted. Eugenie spotted familiar dabs of gold and silver in the structured assembly. Florelle—Solella for tonight—danced with a man in full lion regalia, complete with a massive mane to complement his suede mask. Aurielle—Lunella—gamboled with a brown-feathered eagle whose half-mask extended into a hard yellow beak. With a pang of guilt, Eugenie diverted her path, tracing the balustrade upward to the overlooking balcony instead of joining the sparkling throng.

How she yearned to be in their midst. She'd already betrayed Marielle's trust by coming, though. Watching the spectacle from above would have to suffice.

Women wore garb of every shade and hue, portraying exotic animals, birds, and flowers. The men, most of them, wore the simple domino costume, a black, hooded robe and hat with a white mask. Those who had donned more elaborate guises belonged to the upper elites, their persons dripping with jewels and opulent furs or feathers.

Careful to keep back from the edge of the railing, Eugenie strained for a glimpse of her stepmother. She spied the astral figure near the head of the room, lingering by a pair of doors. The royal thrones stood vacant upon a dais close by.

Had Queen Patrice and her consort Prince Renaud not yet arrived, or did they dance among their guests? Eugenie moved along the balcony, her eyes searching the crowds for any glimpse of their royal persons, or of their son, Prince Fernand.

They weren't there yet. Her heart quickened with anticipation, that she had come in time to witness the royal entrance, and from such a perfect vantage point. Many of the guests pooled toward those double doors. The musicians finished their minuet, and the dancers bowed to one another and clapped their appreciation. Eugenie followed the circle of the balcony, her eyes glued upon the scene below, upon the building anticipation in the crowd.

A row of trumpets sounded a fanfare and the double doors swung open.

She collided with a body walking the opposite direction.

"Oh! I'm so sorry!" she said, mortified as she stepped back.

The victim of her heedlessness, a domino with a full face mask, had caught hold of the balcony to steady himself. "I beg your pardon," he said in equal apology. "I wasn't watching where I was going."

"Neither was I," said Eugenie. She cast a wistful glance below. The queen and prince consort, dressed as a wolf and a lamb, had emerged to a swell of fawning guests, Marielle among them. With a disappointed sigh Eugenie refocused on the domino. "I was looking at the crowds and never thought there might be someone else up here. It's my fault."

His eyes, the only part of his face she could see, crinkled pleasantly behind his mask. "You can't take all the blame. We both blend in with the shadows around us. Although I must say, I never expected to encounter the Queen of the Night up in the rafters."

A laugh burst from her lips. "Queen of the Night? I'm no such thing!"

He took two backward steps, the better to appreciate her smoky, shimmering costume. "Am I mistaken? What else could you be?"

Her lips trembled and her voice shook with repressed mirth. "I'm *soot*." She couldn't stop her smile from manifesting, especially when his eyes widened.

He cobbled his wits together. "That is a *very* imaginative costume. Far more so than a mere domino. Oh, here comes the prince!"

They both swiveled, rapt. Below, behind the queen and her consort, a colorful figure danced into view. Feathers adorned his voluminous sleeves and his cap. His glittering mask had a golden beak attached. The crowd cheered his entrance, and he flapped his hands to their applause.

"He's a popinjay," said Eugenie in wonder. Delight bubbled up her throat.

"That's an imaginative costume too," said the domino, reserve in his voice. The porcelain features of his mask, expressionless, contrasted with the intensity of his gaze on the scene below.

Was he self-conscious about his choice of attire? "But the domino is tradition, isn't it?" she asked.

He favored her with a good-humored glance. "Or laziness."

She tipped her head. "It's efficient."

"And by that, you mean boring."

She could not allow such self-reproach to stand. "No. It allows you to blend in anywhere you like, and to go wherever you want without anyone giving you a second glance." If she could have worn a domino costume—particularly one with a full face mask—she might have gone straight to the dance floor without fear of the Elles recognizing her. But then, she would have had to dance with women all night, because no one expected a domino to dance with one of its own kind.

He turned, propped on one elbow as he faced her. "Do you always put a pleasant spin on everything?"

She blushed. "I'm sorry. It's a habit. I know it's annoying—"

"It's not. Don't apologize, please."

Her embarrassment doubled. Who was this kindly stranger? Florelle had pinched her ear a dozen times for being too positive, and Aurielle always made a horrendous groan of long-suffering. Marielle tolerated it, but with a tightness to her smile that warned Eugenie to keep her thoughts to herself. And she did, most of the time, but the novelty of a masquerade had distracted her.

The domino, aware of her discomfiture, continued the conversation as though nothing were amiss. "I wanted a bird's-eye view for when the royals came in. Look at how everyone flocks to them."

Below, the fawning crowds pressed tight around the ruling family, bowing and chattering compliments and thanks. Marielle grasped the queen's hand and kissed it with obsequies that made Eugenie all the more ashamed for the spectacle.

"Everyone loves them," she said faintly.

The domino crossed his arms and leaned again upon the balustrade, the better to peer over the edge to the riotous scene. "It's odd, don't you think, that the queen is a wolf and her husband is the lamb? Shouldn't it be the other way around?"

He glanced toward her. She joined him, propping her forearms against the railing. "Perhaps he's a wolf in sheep's clothing."

The domino chuckled. "I like that, Milady Night."

"I told you I'm soot."

"Shall I call you Milady Soot, then? But it seems so unfitting for such an impressive costume."

She ruminated on this conundrum. The best costumes always had names attached. Her gaze lit upon Florelle in her gold froth and Aurielle in silver, both of them pushing through the crowds to join their mother, to bow before the lamb and wolf and simper at the popinjay prince.

A smile tugged at Eugenie's lips. "You can call me Cinderella."

The domino's eyes crinkled. "I like that. It's excessively clever."

She surveyed him speculatively. "And shall I call you Pip in return?"

He tipped his head, but the connection between his name and his costume struck an instant later. "There's nothing shared between the costume and the game except the name, you know."

"You're both black and white," she replied.

"True. I must concede, Milady Cinderella. I shall answer to 'Pip,' a woefully plain name to compliment my woefully plain costume."

How could he be so expressive with only his eyes? Every word he spoke seemed in jest.

"Sir Pip, then," she said with a light-hearted chuckle.

He bowed. "You are all benevolence."

The musicians strummed a chord below, signaling another dance to start. The popinjay prince, the master of the dance for tonight, called for couples to take their places in a quadrille. He swooped through the crowds seeking a partner as his parents assumed their positions of authority upon the dais.

Soot and Slipper

"Don't you participate in the festivities, Cinderella?" asked the domino at her side.

"I think I prefer the bird's-eye view," she said, though her heart longed to join the gathering company. To come this far only to watch—! But she shouldn't have come at all, not only because of her stepfamily, but because her fairy benefactor had openly intended mischief. If she stayed out of the way, though, what trouble could she cause? Florelle and Aurielle both had partners lining up with them. Marielle had staked out a place near enough the queen that she could speak with her during the set. Keeping to the shadows seemed Eugenie's lot in life.

"Surely you don't mean to stay up here all night," said Pip.

She spared him a wistful glance and returned her attention to the scene below.

"Curiouser and curiouser," he murmured. "Are you a fairy come to crash the royal festivities?"

Her head jerked. "Of course not," she said, a hitch in her voice.

Her companion laughed, hanging onto the railing in his mirth.

"Do fairies crash these events?" she asked, stricken. Perhaps this was the mischief her "godmother" had meant to stir.

"How should I know? We're all wearing masks."

"Perhaps you're a fairy," she said.

"Perhaps I am. Not an imaginative one, if so."

She snorted, unable to contain her amusement. "You have plenty of charm to make up for it, at least. Why are *you* not down among the crowds?"

He lolled against the balustrade, peering at her with contentment. "Things are more interesting up here."

Warmth pulsed from her heart. A smile curved along her lips as she shifted her attention to the dance below. Her head swayed gently with the rhythm of the music. The dancers joined and parted in a beautiful pattern, their steps light. Gorgeous dresses swished and capes whirled as couples pranced with and around each other. The set came to an end and the popinjay called for a jig, much to the company's approval.

Pip broke the companionable silence. "Don't you want to meet Prince Fernand?" His eyes twinkled behind his mask.

A tinkling laugh escaped Eugenie's lips. "No. I've met him before."

His interest sparked; he leaned closer. "Is that so? When?"

She waved a fluttering hand. "When I was a child. He was a troublemaker, but I never would have branded him a popinjay." She laughed again, her spirits airy as she gazed over the balcony at the colorful prince. He frolicked in his vivid costume, hopping to the lively music while his partner, in an ungainly peacock ensemble, struggled to keep up.

"I wonder if she knows that peahens are all drab and that she's dressed as a man," Eugenie said in contemplation. She slid a sly smile toward Sir Pip but found him examining her instead of the floundering peafowl. Her brows drew together. Had she offended him?

"Where did you meet him?" he asked, more serious than the occasion merited. Apprehension slithered through her, but even as she pulled away from their intimate huddle, his good humor returned on a chuckle. "I mean, do I have the honor of speaking to a high-ranking lady of the court? Shall I be thrashed when it comes time for everyone to remove their masks?"

Her lightheartedness returned. So he was a lesser noble or a peasant, worried of offending one of his betters. But he had no cause for concern. "Oh. No, I'm nothing so extravagant. And I won't be here at the unmasking anyway."

He stood straight. "Why not?" He sounded concerned. Would he look concerned too, if she could see beneath that porcelain façade?

"Because I promised my benefactor I'd be back by midnight," she said, contented resignation curving along her lips. Her heart warmed at the disappointment that emanated from him, that so short an acquaintance could make him lament the loss of her company.

He tried to persuade her. "The party has barely started by midnight. Most of the guests will be here until dawn."

"But I won't be among them." When her words elicited an unhappy tilt of his head, she met his disapproval with reproach. "What sort of ingrate would I be if I didn't keep my promise? If not for my benefactor, I couldn't have come here at all."

His eyes softened behind his mask. "Then allow me to send my compliments to your benefactor." He grasped her gloved hand in his and raised her fingers to his porcelain lips, but they bumped against his chin instead.

Eugenie burst out laughing at the clumsy, endearing gesture. "That's what you get for wearing a full mask."

"Truly I am undone," he replied, though his shoulders shook with mirth. "Madam Cinderella, as your time here is short, what say we make the most of it?"

Her levity subsided. "What do you mean?"

He extended his white-gloved hand. "We cannot occupy the bird's-eye view forever. Come dance with me." The invitation in his sparkling eyes beckoned her, but she tamped down her soaring heart.

"I don't dance. I only meant to watch."

"I'll lead you. No one will spare us a second glance in that crush."

Wistfully she checked the floor below. Florelle and Aurielle swirled among the throng, each partnered with a lord in an extravagant costume, while their mother flirted with a demonic monstrosity along the edge of the ballroom.

Even if they recognized her, surely they wouldn't begrudge her dancing with a lowly domino.

Hesitantly she placed her hand in his. Warmth spread up her arm as he guided her to the balcony stairs. Guests lined the lower steps, conversing. The pair wove a threaded path through them to the density of bodies on the ballroom floor. The popinjay prince called for a spinner, and the musicians picked up their pace. Before she could breathe, Sir Pip looped an arm around her waist and careened them together into the lively, bouncing dance.

Sheer and utter joy tumbled from her lips. They were gliding, flying as the music circled in a rising cadence. She closed her eyes and tipped back her head, relishing in the thrill of the moment. She and her domino spun together like two cinders carried upward on a gust of smoke.

The song ended, and the prince called for a nizzarda. Their steps shifted to the energetic dance. She laughed and pranced and swung in Pip's arms, and all the while he smiled at her from behind his porcelain mask.

The set ended all too soon. Breathless, she joined the rest of the company in a roar of applause. On the opposite side of the ballroom, the prince in his feathered mutton sleeves raised his hands and called for a more sedate minuet.

Her domino tugged her toward an open pavilion, and she willingly left the crush behind.

"You do dance," he said when his voice could be heard above the din.

"Only country dances," she replied, her smile still in full force. "You're lucky I didn't trample your feet."

"You're light as a feather. I doubt I'd have felt it."

"My slippers are made of glass. You'd be lucky to escape with only a bruise."

He peered down, impressed, for a glimpse of the obsidian shoes beneath her voluminous skirts. "Those can't be comfortable."

"They are," said Eugenie, beaming. "I feel like I'm walking on a cloud."

"So do I, but it's not because of my shoes."

Though the crowd thinned around them, he kept his fingers intertwined with hers until shyly she drew back her hand. He didn't seem to notice, or if he did, he took no offense.

"Are you thirsty?" he asked. "The air is closer down here than in the balcony, and I think I might die for lack of refreshment."

A glass of cold water sounded like heaven, but another concern trumped this desire. "How will you drink anything in such a mask?" she asked, her eyes sparkling with mirth.

"I'll take it off, of course."

Her brows arched. "Is that allowed?"

"Oh, I won't do it here where everyone can see. I'll stand in a corner where no one pays me any attention. No one looks twice at a mere domino, as you so aptly said."

Her delight mirrored his own. Together they traced a path back to the refreshments on an outside concourse. Not a drop of water graced the food-laden tables, but the palace had provided wine and a frothy, sparkly punch. Sir Pip poured a cup of the latter and offered it to her.

"Is it . . . ?" She bit her lower lip. Marielle always cautioned her girls against imbibing, that such an act could impair a lady's faculties and thus lead to her disgrace.

"Nothing strong," he said, reading her concern, "only fruit juice and cream blended together."

She accepted the delicate cup and sniffed at its contents. The sweet smell matched Pip's description. "How do you know that's all?"

He poured himself a glass, holding the ladle high so that a pink stream flowed from its edge to the cup. "It's a popular drink among the upper-class ladies. I heard the queen has guards stationed to watch the tables so no one can embellish on it. The wine's not strong either. No one wants any sullen drunks in their company tonight."

Eugenie huffed a laugh into her cup, grateful she hadn't been swallowing at that precise moment. The sweet flavor of the punch filled her senses on the first long sip—truly the signature taste of a wonderful party.

"You have me at an advantage," said Pip, holding his full glass.

"I beg your pardon. I thought you meant to abandon me so you could remove your mask."

"Why should I abandon you? Or perhaps you're ready to abandon me. You can, though I shall lament that moment and every one thereafter."

"You are absurd," she said with a laugh. "Where is your secretive corner, then, that we can retreat?"

Again his eyes crinkled. He tipped his head and led the way along the wall toward the broad gardens. In a shadowed alcove sat a small table and two chairs with full view of the mingling crowds. Pip set down his cup at one place and pulled the chair opposite for Eugenie. She sank to it, her curious eyes upon him.

He crossed around to the other side of the table, his back to the crowds and his face obscured by the darkness around them. When he reached toward his mask, he paused.

Soot and Slipper

"Promise you won't laugh?"

Her inability to meet this demand trembled on her lips, but she nodded. Did he have some disfigurement that required the full mask? His form beneath the cape was normal enough, and his energy in dancing had proven at least an average physique. Perhaps he was a spry old man, with wrinkles patterned across his skin.

He didn't *sound* old.

He unfastened the mask. Her breath caught in her throat as he pulled it aside to reveal—

A second half-mask beneath.

She burst into a peal of mirth. This was, perhaps, the greatest joke of the night.

4
Embers Alight

"I HAD TO PLAN for all my options," said Sir Pip, and he took a modest sip of his punch while Eugenie recovered her wits. Just when she had the laughter under control, his grinning face started her into another bout.

Tears formed at the corners of her eyes. "I'm so sorry. I didn't—"

"You didn't expect such genius from a lowly domino. I know. Sir Pip has triumphantly surprised his Cinderella."

She liked the casual possessive that he spoke. She liked his face, too, what she could see of it: an elegant jaw and a charming smile. His eyes were brown, and they were so pleasant and expressive that she might stare into them captivated for hours.

But Marielle's voice spoke a warning in her ears, of how important it was for a lady never to form quick attachments. A gentleman's temperament could appear pleasant one evening and cruel the following day. He might pretend good fortune when he was a wastrel and a spendthrift. His true character could be more of a ruse than the full mask that hid a half-one.

Ruthlessly she thrust the warnings aside. This was a

masquerade. No one was who they pretended to be, not even her. For one night she could ignore such worries and enjoy the moment. She wasn't likely to see him ever again.

They ate a light supper together and laughed over absurd subjects. From their vantage point, they observed the other guests, costumes from the mundane to the fantastic. Eugenie, enraptured, noted all the embellishments and variable patterns that she could, mentally cataloguing and dissecting their constructs.

When they finished their meal and people-watching, Pip hid his full mask beneath a flowering shrub and asked her to dance with him again. "I'll come back for it later in the night," he said when she expressed her concern. "No one will find it, and if they do, it's not much for me to procure another one."

They spun upon the ballroom floor, traded partners, and returned to one another. They visited the card tables for a quick rubber of whist, which they lost spectacularly. "Better keep to the dance," Pip said with a wink, and she laughingly agreed.

Her spirit exulted in the energy of the fete, in the joy of participating in everything. When the clock chimed eleven-thirty, her heart was full to its brim.

Sir Pip saw her glance toward the majestic timepiece. Though his smile faded, he led her from the crush of rollicking dancers toward the palace courtyard, where the carriages awaited their guests.

"Will you come to another masquerade?" he asked, a note of wistfulness in his voice.

Eugenie peeked at him from the corners of her eyes, her view partially obscured by the edges of her mask. Rather than give the hard negative she ought, she said, "Thank you so much for tonight. It was wonderful, more so than I expected." Her heart fluttered with regret that she could not stay longer. A scant few hours had filled her soul and left it strangely empty at the same time.

"The pleasure was wholly mine, Milady," said Pip, and he bowed low over her black-gloved hand. As he straightened again, their eyes locked. Longing, anticipation, delight all jittered within her.

Why did she have to go? Oh, yes, the fairy. Her beautiful gown would melt away, and then her charming companion would see her in her threadbare work dress, with a tattered apron and her hair tied up in a lanky tail instead of lovely ringlets.

She'd rather not face his inevitable disappointment.

Sir Pip's voice lowered to an intimate hush. "I wonder—and I recognize my impertinence in this..."

"Hmm?" Eugenie prompted.

A smile touched the corners of his lips. He paused but then pressed forward. "If I kissed you, would I come away with ashes on my mask?"

A flock of butterflies converged upon her heart. Memories—she could take memories alone from this wonderful night. Even if she never saw him again, she would have a lovely memory to cherish. She tempered her answer to sound light, airy, careless.

"There's only one way to find out."

His brows arched, proof of his uncertainty in making such a bold request. He glanced self-consciously behind them, checking that no one noticed them on the shadowed courtyard stairs. The guards at the doors had moved inward to observe the party. The liverymen below huddled in groups playing cards and throwing dice. No one paid the dark-clad pair a second glance.

Pip leaned in. His mouth brushed against hers, almost reverential. Sunshine blossomed within her at the contact. She slid light fingers against his jaw and answered the kiss in kind. He deepened it, pulling her close, but the noses of their half-masks caught and obstructed any further connection. They parted on a mutual laugh, like two children tangled in a happy game.

"It has been a pleasure, Sir Pip," she said, cradling his face in her hands. "And no ashes whatsoever on your cheeks."

He closed his fingers around hers, his warmth traveling through their gloves. "I might as well go home too. This party is over for me as soon as you leave."

She delighted in the compliment but deflected it all the same. "Nonsense. There are a hundred more girls in there for you to kiss. I trust you to make a full night of it, since I cannot."

His expression immediately sobered. "I would never—"

The clock chimed the quarter-hour. "I'm late," Eugenie said, drawing back. At the base of the stairs, her vine-and-shadow carriage awaited, the frog-horses pawing the ground in restless compulsion.

"Cinderella—" her domino began as she stepped away.

"Goodnight, Sir Pip," she said, a brilliant smile fixed upon her face. "May good fortune smile upon you!"

She hurried down the steps, to where the shadowed footman held her carriage door. Gingerly she climbed inside, and only when she settled back into the cushions did she allow herself a final glance. The carriage lurched into motion. Her domino stood frozen halfway up the stairs, forlorn as he watched her leave.

Tears tumbled down her cheeks from beneath her mask. She wiped them quickly away, forcing a smile in their stead. "How lucky I have been," she said as his figure blended into the shadows and the staircase moved beyond her line of sight.

All she'd wanted was one evening at a party. She'd fallen in love instead. Certainly it was fleeting, doomed to end as soon as it began, but she guarded the precious moments jealously close to her heart.

Marielle would scold if she ever found out. A lady didn't kiss a gentlemen the first evening she met him, and certainly not a gentleman whose real name she didn't even know.

But perhaps Pip wasn't a gentleman at all. Perhaps he was a servant who had come to play among his masters, or a tradesman, or a highwayman. Perhaps he was an impoverished nobleman forced to wait until his majority to come into his rightful inheritance. They might have everything in common, or nothing at all.

She laughed, caught halfway between elation and despair.

"Fairy mischief indeed," she said with a tearful smile. How could this new attachment be so dear and so painful at the same time? Such exquisite opposition squeezed her heart as though it were a sponge.

The mischief magnified a mile from home. The midnight hour struck and the glamour upon her carriage and costume melted into fairy dust, as forewarned. She tumbled from phantom cushions to the dirt road, though the de-transformation cradled her to the very end. She picked herself up amid half a dozen displaced pond frogs. With a chuckle, she gathered the creatures into her apron and completed her journey home.

She passed through the fence posts at long last. A patchwork of stars behind the manor house highlighted its looming silhouette. She deposited the frogs in their pond and started toward the front door.

"I warned you it would end at midnight," said the fairy's disembodied voice.

"I know," said Eugenie. "Thank you very much."

"You had a good time?"

"Oh, yes. It was wonderful."

"Of course it was. I only do wonderful things."

She allowed a breathy laugh and hurried inside, wary of betraying more than necessary to the supernatural creature. Within the front room, she stoked a fire from the banked coals in the grate and curled up with a blanket. The evening played upon her thoughts like a dream, culminating in that blissful moment on the stairs.

"A pox on half-masks," Eugenie murmured as she drifted off to sleep. Her domino's face swam before her, his eyes earnest and his mouth curved in a smile. For all they had shared, she might not recognize him in a public place. She'd recognize his voice, though, of that she was sure.

Providing that a night's rest didn't fade her memories like it did all of her other dreams, into oblivion.

5
Slow Burn

"I want a pink dress."

Eugenie looked up from the patterns strewn across her workroom table.

Florelle plopped into the chair just within the door, her hooked nose pulled upward in a sneer. "There were so many colorful dresses last night, and I was stuck in boring gold."

"Your costume was beautiful," said Eugenie, mystified. The sun, moon, and stars had held their own place among the masqueraders. No one would have guessed that an impoverished nobleman's daughter had created them instead of a proper seamstress.

"It was *boring*," said Florelle with a peevish scowl. "You would know if you had seen what everyone else wore. I want pink, something exotic and wonderful."

A smile tugged at Eugenie's mouth. "Like a flamingo?"

Florelle, over-sensitive about her gangly neck, glowered.

"A rose, then?" Eugenie asked, quickly covering her mistake. "Do you have a pink dress to donate? I can't make three costumes from nothing in only a week."

"Can you make a rose?" her stepsister asked, suspicious.

"Probably. I'd need a lot of ribbon."

A clatter sounded from the hall. Aurielle hung upon the door jamb, half-frantic. "If she's going as a rose, I want to be one too!"

"No, Aurie!" Florelle leapt from her chair, furious.

"Why should you get the prettiest flower?"

"You look *terrible* in pink! And we can't both be the same thing, you unimaginative cow!"

Aurielle gasped like an injured thespian.

"Girls, girls!" Marielle appeared, pushing herself between the pair before they could tear each other's hair out. "What on earth has triggered such an unladylike scene?"

Aurielle flung an accusing finger at her stepsister. "It's Eugenie's fault! She's going to make Florelle a prettier costume than mine, *again*!"

Astonished, Eugenie opened her mouth to defend herself. Florelle interjected before a single word could leave her lips.

"You think the *sun* was a better costume than the moon? I felt like a brazen idiot all night long while you were dancing in your silvery best! And everyone said that Mother's was the most beautiful costume of the night."

Marielle, in the midst of keeping her girls separate, fought a rising blush.

"Not everyone," said Aurielle, oblivious to her mother's pleasure. "There was that girl who disappeared. Everyone called her the Queen of the Night, and her costume was so beautiful that I wanted to cry. She put us *all* to shame."

"She only danced with a domino until they disappeared together," said Florelle in utter scorn. "What's the use of having a beautiful costume if you're going to duck out early?"

Eugenie's breath caught in her throat, her body frozen lest she draw anyone's attention. They had noticed her? Even though she kept to the common crowds? Surely they wouldn't begrudge her if they knew the truth.

"Now, girls," said Marielle, shaking off her delicate fingertips as though expelling dust. "There's no sense in fixating on an obvious commoner."

"Her costume wasn't common," said Florelle.

"Her manner was," Marielle replied, a thorn in her cultured voice. "Dancing with the same man so many times? At an unmasked ball, such behavior would be a scandal even if they were married. At a masquerade, it only passed because there were so many dominos in the crowd. She *might* have changed partners, though it's almost certain she did not. And that she disappeared with him so early in the night does not speak volumes for her virtue."

Eugenie, the unwitting subject of this condemnation, wished to sink into the floor. "I'm sure it was all very innocent," she said in a faint voice.

Her stepmother's attention snapped to her face, and the severity around her lips cracked into a smile. "Oh, you sweet child, so unversed in the ways of the world. Perhaps it was innocent, as you say, but I suspect not. Rakes and libertines abound at a masquerade, ready to prey upon unsuspecting females. Her costume really was lovely, though. I wish you could have seen it."

The compliment fell flat as the kiss on the staircase flashed into Eugenie's mind. Her guilt magnified. Was Sir Pip a libertine? Was she only the first in a string of conquests he made last night?

The lovely memory turned to ash. Had she not challenged him to kiss other girls? But she hadn't believed he would, even shrouded in anonymity as they both were.

"That's not to say the costumes you made were any less beautiful," said her stepmother, misreading her dismay. "I had so many compliments I couldn't keep track of them. Florelle and Aurielle never went without a partner, all the way up to the unmasking. Everyone asked for the name of our seamstress, and we delighted in withholding our little secret."

"Even the prince himself complimented us, and he was dressed as the most outlandish popinjay you've ever seen," said Aurielle smugly.

"But a popinjay doesn't pair well with the sun!" Florelle stamped her foot. "I want to match the prince!"

"He certainly won't dress as a popinjay again," her mother said, but she was beyond reason.

"I want a pink dress! I want to be a rose! Eugenie said she could make me a rose, and I don't want Aurielle ruining it!"

Her sister's face screwed up into a sneer. "Your taste is in your mouth, Florie. You wouldn't know a good costume if it strangled you. Why shouldn't I be a rose? A lovely white one!"

They lunged at one another's throats, and Marielle separated them again with a reproving glance toward her stepdaughter. "Eugenie, I wish you would've consulted me before making promises."

"I didn't—"

"Girls, if you can't come to some agreement, neither of you will go as a rose. And Aurielle, you know that pure white makes your complexion turn swarthy. You're much better suited for jewel colors."

"Ha!" Florelle crowed in triumph.

"I want to go as rubies, then," said Aurielle with a flash of menace. "A lovely, deep red ruby!"

Her mother opened and shut her mouth, the blood draining from her face.

"I could probably manage something like that," said Eugenie, recalling her jet-and-onyx bodice from the night before. "If we could find enough colored glass, I mean."

Three pairs of eyes turned on her. Florelle looked as though her world had caved in, while Aurielle puffed up with hope. Marielle bit her lower lip.

"And if we have a red dress to start from," Eugenie said, already engulfed in a creative trance. She scribbled in her open sketchbook a bodice pieced with broken glass. It would have to be a structured garment, far more difficult than the ribbon-roses of Florelle's requested design.

"A rose and rubies," said her stepmother, barely above a whisper. "And what would you dress me in?"

Eugenie jolted from her sketch, her eyes huge upon the petite woman, whose expression was closed, unreadable. "What would you like to go as?" she asked, hesitant.

"I don't know. Surprise me."

A shiver ran down Eugenie's spine. Marielle, usually the sweetest of women, sometimes exuded a bloodless aura that could quell even the most stalwart of hearts. She gathered her daughters to her, ushering them toward the hall.

"What about a raven?" Eugenie asked.

Her stepmother paused on the threshold, a question in her eyes. "Because it starts with the same letter as rose and ruby?"

Eugenie kept her voice neutral, her pulse quickening in her throat. "Because it would complete the set: animal, vegetable, mineral. And because you look lovely in black—a rich blue-black, with feathers and beading."

They had plenty of black dresses to choose from, too, though she forbore from adding this detail.

"It sounds interesting," said Marielle. "We've seen for ourselves how lovely a black costume can be, and as the mother of two other guests, I can hardly wear a bright color. I look forward to seeing the finished product." With nothing else, she led her daughters from the workroom, leaving Eugenie to her scraps and sketches.

A raven, a rose, and a ruby. She wiped her brow with the back of her wrist and scribbled a list of necessities into her book. If last week's work was difficult, this week's might be near impossible.

Time passed all too quickly. Eugenie spent her days from sunrise to late night dyeing and cutting and sewing. Marielle found some cast-off panes of red glass at the flea market in town. They smashed nicely, but their sharp edges would slice through any binding threads. Eugenie spent an afternoon in their derelict farmhouse, wearing down shards on the old grindstone there. She sewed the polished results onto a blood-red bodice that sparkled like a many-faceted jewel.

Florelle's requested rose required two dresses instead of one, so that the costume's skirt could layer into drooping petals. Luckily, the girls had gone through a period where their mother had dressed them in the same colors. The pale pink had not suited Aurielle, but getting her to donate the second gown was still a fight. In the evenings Eugenie sewed ribbons into dozens of rosettes and attached them in clusters at the shoulders, the waist, and at gathers upon the skirt.

The masks, pink and red satin, had embellishments of cut glass and more rosettes. She called the two costumes "Corunella" and "Rhodella." Her stepmother's raven, "Branella," lagged behind in its construction.

"As long as my girls have something to wear, it's no matter if mine gets done," Marielle said as the days progressed. But she also checked the status of her costume every afternoon when she stopped by to make sure her stepdaughter had eaten.

Raven feathers they had none. Eugenie used chicken quills instead and steeped them in a vat of black dye. Her stepmother had worn mourning clothes for a full two years after Eugenie's father passed away. Within her wardrobe was a lovely black-satin gown that needed little alteration to render it perfect for a masquerade. Black beading added some extra embellishment, and a plumed mask and headdress completed the ensemble.

Eugenie barely finished in time. When the last feather was in place—on the very afternoon of the masquerade, no less—Marielle surveyed the black gown with a glint of satisfaction in her eyes.

"You really are a wonder," she said, and Eugenie blushed. Marielle favored her with an apologetic smile. "I do wish you could come as well. If they gave us more time between these events, you might make yourself a costume."

Surprised by her stepmother's seeming change of heart, she said, "I could always go as the sun, moon, or stars."

"Oh, no," said Marielle, scandalized. "To wear a second-hand costume? Everyone would know who you were, and they would know we couldn't afford to get you something of your own. How could I bear it if you had to suffer such indignity?"

To which Eugenie only smiled and surmised that her stepmother didn't want her there after all. But it was nice of her to pretend.

Florelle and Aurielle shoved their way into the workroom, preventing any further conversation. They squabbled over whose dress was prettier and carried away the mounds of fabric to their own rooms, manhandling the exquisite constructions as they went. Marielle, more careful with her own disguise, paused in the doorway.

"We'll make it up to you, somehow," she said, her voice wistful. "At least you'll have a quiet evening all to yourself."

Eugenie nodded, not trusting herself to speak. Disappointment lodged in her throat, against her wishes. She had attended last week's party, after all. She had no cause for resentment or dismay.

Still, there were three perfectly beautiful costumes she might choose from, should Marielle but allow it. Even second-hand, they would serve her better than staying home alone.

She squashed the desire. It was imperative for Florelle and Aurielle to find husbands, and one less rival would increase their chances for success. Besides, she'd already disgraced herself once. Obviously she couldn't be trusted at a masquerade.

The three Elles piled into their hired carriage, chattering like hens. As usual, Eugenie watched until they passed beyond the fence posts to the main road.

As usual, they never looked back.

With a deflated sigh, she turned to the house.

"Aren't you going again tonight?" asked the ethereal fairy from the direction of the garden.

Anticipation thrummed through her, but she tamped it down. Certainly she had wondered whether the creature would appear again, and she had dreamed all week of meeting Sir Pip despite her apparent disgrace. She had had her fun once already, though. Tempting fate a second time could bring dire consequences.

"I don't think it's a good idea," she said. When she started up the stairs to the door, a flash of light arrested her. The fiery-headed fairy blocked her path.

"Don't be silly. A party is always a good idea."

Eugenie, much inclined to agree, swallowed that instinct. "I went last week. I don't want to draw more attention than I already have."

"Do you think you were born to waste away on this estate, where no one but your chickens can ever see you? Listen to your heart and let your godmother dress you up. You deserve a party after all the work you've done, if only for the dinner you might have there."

Eugenie cast a wistful glance in the direction of the kitchen, where a stale quarter-loaf of bread and some sour milk awaited her. She might go to the party, eat her fill of good food, and come home immediately afterward. There was no rule that said she had to stay until midnight, or that she even had to dance.

"And what will you dress me up as tonight?" she asked, curious. "Is it animal, vegetable, or mineral?"

"None of those," said the fairy with a beneficent smile. "You'll go as the force that consumes them all. Embers, my little Eugenie—embers to stoke a bright and vibrant fire."

Suddenly, more than anything, Eugenie wanted to see what a costume of embers would look like. She fairly itched for it.

"All right, then. I thank you kindly for your help."

"And I thank you kindly for your mischief." The fairy punctuated these ominous words with a smug wink. Eugenie, already ensnared, cast aside her worries and let the transformation proceed.

6
Innocence in Flames

Vermillion flared against black, sparkling like live coals carried into the night sky. The bottom of Eugenie's costume was fiery red, but it bled upward into darkness. Those jeweled embers—red, orange, and white—scattered up the skirt and onto the bodice in stark contrast. Her hair, piled in curls atop her head, had a gemstone clip to hold it into place, and her mask was veined with glittering orange against velvety black. The whole costume shimmered, dazzling to the eye.

She took a deep breath as she left the shadowed confines of her phantom carriage and hitched her skirts, the red of her evening gloves so dark that they were almost inky. Her slippers, cut from smoky quartz tonight, clacked against the marble staircase as she climbed, their fit no less comfortable than their obsidian predecessors.

Her heart soared with the music on the air, though anxiety swelled in her windpipe.

She would go straight into the crowds tonight. She would eat a good dinner among the other ladies of the court and dance with as many different partners as would ask her. If Pip was in the throng, she would not seek him out nor pay him any special notice should he find her.

All this she had decided during the carriage ride. Her reputation—even as a masquerader—depended on her conduct. She would cause no disgrace to herself or anyone else tonight.

Even so, she hesitated on the palace threshold. Only when the guards at the door slid inquiring glances toward her did she steel her nerves and pass inside.

Straight to the dance floor. Straight to the dance floor. She approached the stairs to the grand hall. From the path that led up to the balcony, a tumult of footsteps clattered.

Startled, Eugenie paused. Her heart spasmed in her chest as a domino in full face mask bolted downward as though to intercept her. He halted six feet away, his brown eyes huge upon her.

Words would not come. Neither would her feet move.

Had he been watching for her?

Pip swept into a low bow. "I beg your deepest pardon, Milady."

No special notice. She'd promised herself.

"Do I know you?" said Eugenie in arch hauteur, but the desire to favor him quickened her heartbeat.

Her domino dared lift his gaze. The full mask hid his reaction to her impertinent question, but his voice rang out in respectful tones. "I am your humble servant."

She hummed, as if considering. "That doesn't sound right."

"Please, Cinderella, if you will but forgive my impertinence when last we met—" His voice arrested in his throat. He straightened, examining her wondrous costume. "But you are not Cinderella tonight, I suppose."

She could not fully rebuff him. Her partiality surfaced in the upward curve of her mouth. "The name should still suffice. I've only gone from soot to embers."

Her eyes met his, and an electric shock thrummed up her spine. What need had she for a reputation? She had done nothing very bad.

"I should not have taken the liberties I did," said Pip. He fiddled with the fingertips of his gloves, watching for her response. "I did not consider anything beyond the pleasure of the moment. When I realized what damage I may have caused, to your feelings and your reputation both, I was in agony—have been in agony ever since. Can you forgive me?"

The apology was both sweet and disappointing. To hear him speak with regrets about an occasion they had both delighted in only confirmed her fears. She was in disgrace.

But a rake would never apologize for such behavior. At least she could rest her mind on that count.

"You took no liberties I did not allow, Sir Pip," she said, her voice a gentle cadence. "The fault was mine as much as yours." Gracefully she hitched her skirt a degree and started toward the stairs, but his jerking movement arrested her once more.

He was rigid, one hand half-raised. Concern emanated from him. "Am I forgiven?"

"There is nothing to forgive," she said.

"Then may I keep you company again tonight? I swear I will behave like a perfect gentleman."

She glanced to the dancing throng below, her heart torn between desire and decorum. Of course he was no libertine. Two seconds in his presence would convince anyone as much.

Yet still, Marielle's condemnation rang in her ears. She chose her words carefully. "I am told it is improper for a lady and a gentleman to keep company with only one another at such a gathering."

"I was reminded of that as well," said Pip. The formality of his words broke into frankness. "It's a terrible rule, Cinderella. I don't want anyone else's company if I might have yours."

Warmth blossomed in her ribcage and spread to her extremities. Pink with delight, she opened her mouth to reply, but she didn't get the chance.

"Good evening, Milady Flame," said a crocodile coming up the stairs. He bowed low, though he kept his eyes fixed upon Eugenie behind his scaled mask. "Might I request your hand for the next set?"

Pip stepped forward in haste, as though to block the newcomer's further approach. "She is my dance partner." He looked to Eugenie for confirmation, a silent plea in his eyes.

The masquerader on the stairs stiffened, his shoulders going taut and his eyes narrowing. Before he could challenge Pip's claim, she lowered into a deep curtsy.

"I beg your pardon," she said to the crocodile. "The gentleman is correct. I am already engaged to dance with him, but I thank you for the honor of your request."

Relief flashed through Sir Pip's eyes.

"Another time, Milady." The crocodile bowed and retreated.

Pip caught her gloved hand in his. "You are the most gracious of souls."

"Or simply," she said, squeezing his fingers, "I find I don't want anyone else's company if I might have yours."

She descended to the ballroom floor on his arm, and they joined the forming sets. The royals had not yet arrived, so the prince was not there to call the dance. Instead the orchestra played a stately minuet, and the dancers followed their lead.

To Eugenie's eyes, Pip was the only person there. The others were mere phantoms that circled in and around her as the set progressed.

Soot and Slipper

The illusion broke when the music stopped. Half a dozen costumed men flocked to her to beg the next dance. She gaped, flustered, but Pip looped a protective arm around her waist.

"She is *my* dance partner," he said, almost belligerent in his claim. Teeth set on edge and shoulders stiffened, but their protests drowned in a blast of trumpets. The double doors at the head of the room opened, and a herald announced the arrival of the queen and prince consort—dressed as a cat and mouse, respectively—followed by their son in the garb of a vibrant goldfish, complete with a fish-faced mask that covered his eyes and nose. He waved webbed gloves above his head as he pranced into the room, his sleeves voluminous orange fins.

How disappointed Florelle would be. Roses and goldfish didn't mix any better than the sun and a parrot.

Nobility surged to offer their obsequies and commoners cheered for Prince Fernand's unorthodox costume choice. In the distraction, Pip whisked Eugenie from among her crowd of admirers. They stole through to the courtyard, where early diners flocked the buffet of fine foods.

"Are you hungry?" Pip asked.

"Famished," said Eugenie, though her soaring spirits seemed fare enough to satisfy any appetite.

"What say we grab a plate and sneak away to the balcony for a picnic? Or would you rather take your chances with the crowds?"

Much as she loved the energy of the masquerade, the abundance of would-be partners had overwhelmed her. Seclusion was a far better option. The abandoned balcony would draw no attention while allowing them to people-watch.

They collected their dinners and skulked through the shadows, back into the palace and up the stairs. "Will we get in trouble?" Eugenie whispered when they slipped up onto the balcony.

"No. A domino can go wherever he pleases without anyone looking twice at him." He punctuated this statement with a wink.

She chuckled.

The dancing continued below. They settled on the floor next to the balustrade, able to peer between the gaps at the spectacle while remaining hidden from notice. Eugenie, nestled amid voluminous skirts, arranged herself into a modest position. Her faceted shoes poked out from the edge of her hem.

They caught Sir Pip's eye. "Glass slippers again?"

"Quartz tonight," she said, peering over the folds of her dress to glimpse them.

"The workmanship is exquisite. A gift from your benefactor?"

"Yes." Her gown was her own dress magicked into a different form, but the slippers were woven from pure fairy dust. Her worn shoes remained at home, awaiting her return in a patch of grass by the stairs to the manor house because the fairy deemed them too shabby to transform.

"And I suppose you have to make an early exit tonight again," he said with reservation.

She nodded, brimming with unspoken regret.

A sigh of long-suffering escaped him. He reached up and removed the full face mask, revealing the half-mask beneath again. "Then I shall soak up your warmth while I can and hope it sustains me until we meet again. Who is this benefactor who tortures me so?"

Eugenie conveniently popped a bite of her dinner roll into her mouth.

Pip quirked a smile. "That's all right. I didn't expect an answer."

Soot and Slipper

They chattered as they ate—light, nonsensical conversation. After they finished, Pip stacked their dishes next to the wall with a promise to clear them once she had gone. He stood and offered her both hands. She took them, and he pulled her up as though she were weightless.

"Shall we venture down again, or would you rather stay up here a while longer?"

It wasn't even ten o'clock. Although tempted by the dance, she could hardly justify keeping Pip as her exclusive partner should they return. In the balcony, no one could judge them for remaining in one another's company.

She wandered to the balustrade, fascinated by the patterns of movement below. "The colors are so much darker tonight," she said as she leaned over the railing. From above, the trend was more apparent: more women had opted for blacks and blues and indigos in their choice of dress than last week. She tried to discern Marielle among them, but wherever she was, she blended in.

An apprehensive lump rose in her throat. Eugenie swallowed it, wary of having caused her stepmother injury by giving her a costume that fit in with others instead of standing out.

Beside her, Pip let out a grunt of satisfaction. "No doubt that was the influence of last week's Queen of the Night." She looked to him sharply. His smile only broadened. "You must know yours was the most beautiful costume of the masquerade. As it is tonight."

"Surely not." The words escaped in a faint protest. She returned her attention to the dancing crowd, conscious of a blush that swept up her neck to her face. "As for dark colors, someone else was dressed as a starry sky. You can't say my influence was more than hers."

"Baroness Lavande," he said, peering over the balustrade. Eugenie jerked at the name, her stepmother's former title from her first marriage. She opened her mouth to correct him—Marielle was the Marchioness of Pluterra, or the Dowager Marchioness now that the Marquis had died—but she checked herself. Would knowledge of the family give her identity away?

Pip continued, oblivious to her internal struggle. "Her last costume was a fine piece, to be sure, and tonight's is even more so." He pointed into the crowd. "You see the raven there?"

She followed the line of his finger and picked out Marielle's feathered headdress atop her silvery-blonde curls. A crowd of admiring nobles clustered around her.

"Even she has gone from spangled midnight blue to black, though," said Pip. "That's a follower, not a leader. Your influence was profound."

Her breath left her on a shuddering exhale. "I don't believe it."

"Why not?" he asked, all good humor. "Was your surge of suitors tonight not proof enough?"

She spared him a perturbed glance and returned her attention to the dance. "I'm starting to think I really should have stayed home."

"I'm very glad you didn't," said Pip, lounging against the rail so that his view was entirely upon her instead of the crowd.

Eugenie fought the warmth that blossomed within her. She focused stubbornly on the other masqueraders. "The dark costumes make the colorful ones stand out all the more. That pink one there is lovely. Is it a rose?"

She had, of course, picked out Florelle in the middle of a quadrille. Her costume, at least, could draw no complaint.

Pip straightened. "Ah, yes. That's one of the baroness's daughters, though I couldn't say which. Perhaps she meant for them

Soot and Slipper

to shine while she receded into the background tonight. The other is over there, in the vibrant red." He pointed out Aurielle, oblivious that Eugenie was already well attuned to her location.

"What is she dressed as?" she asked, all innocence.

"The most innovative of designs: a ruby. I'm sure both of their costumes will have influence for next week's fete, though not as much as the embers that briefly danced among them."

Determined to ignore the hint, she said firmly, "How did you recognize them?"

"I saw them arrive with the baroness, and she must always be recognized."

"Well, neither of them lack partners. Nor shall they for the whole night, I'd wager."

"They wouldn't." A cynical pitch entered his voice. "Fortune-hunters abound in this crowd, and one of them is set to inherit a sizable estate."

Eugenie frowned at this misinformation, at the trouble it might cause Florelle and Aurielle. "I understood the late Baron Lavande's estate to be quite wasted."

"Not the Lavande estate," said Pip. "The Pluterra one, from their mother's second marriage."

"Oh, no." The words left her lips on instinct. "They can't inherit that one. It belongs to the marquis's natural daughter."

He shifted his gaze to her, his lips parted and his eyes narrowed behind his mask.

"I-it belongs to his natural daughter," Eugenie said again. "She inherits when she comes of age."

But he only shook his head, his mouth a solemn slant. "The Marquis of Pluterra's natural daughter died three years ago."

Shock, cold and jarring, tumbled over her. She forced a smile, clearing her head to keep her wits about her. "You are mistaken."

His expression remained grave. "I'm not. I attended her funeral."

The words made no sense. She took a halting backward step, her gaze unfocused. "You can't have—"

"I did. Everyone did, the whole country over, as a sign of respect for her family. You must have been abroad at the time, not to have known."

What nonsense was this?

"She was the last of the Pluterra line," Pip said, wistfulness in his far-off expression. "The title returned to the crown when she died, and the estate went to the baroness, as the marquis's surviving spouse."

An inelegant noise escaped her throat. She couldn't breathe, couldn't force her lungs to inhale or her mind to work beyond the picture he constructed.

"Cinderella, are you all right?" he asked, reaching for her in concern.

"I have to go," Eugenie said. She flung away from him, her stomach twisting.

"Wait!" He dogged her footsteps. "Cinderella, wait, please."

She paid him no heed, desperate to escape the sudden, stifling heat that threatened to suffocate her. Her walk quickened to a run. She passed the entrance to the cool night air, but there was no relief.

"Cinderella," said Pip, keeping pace beside her. When he reached for her arm, she wrenched away. Anguish played across his face, but she could not remain here even for him.

"I have to go. I'm so sorry. I have to." She picked up her skirts and ran for the grand staircase. Near the top, she stumbled. One of her slippers skittered away, too far out of her path, and in her frenzy to be gone, she left it.

Soot and Slipper

Her carriage, as though sensing her every thought, waited at the base of the stairs. The fairy-footman opened the door, and she threw herself inside, where she kicked off her other shoe.

Stricken, she cast her gaze back toward the stairs as the carriage lurched.

Pip had followed her only as far as the top step. He stooped and carefully picked up the quartz slipper. A tortured breath caught in her throat, but she forced it out. The delicate shoe would disintegrate into fairy dust at midnight. Thank heavens the finicky fairy had not magicked her real shoes with a glamour.

But shoes were the least of her worries.

The ride home passed in a blur, her mind ablaze. The carriage clattered into the yard of her father's estate—of Marielle's estate?—and stopped in the patch of ground between the house and the garden. Her trembling hands slipped from the door latch. She caught it again and shoved it open, almost tumbling from the phantom carriage to the earth. She righted herself, her lovely, voluminous dress rustling around her.

Everything was as she had left it.

And yet, everything had changed.

Numb, sick with disbelief, she started toward the house.

"You're home early." The fairy's voice floated toward her from the garden.

Eugenie halted, ice shooting through her veins. "Yes," she said, her voice hollow.

"And how was the party?" The creature was drifting closer. Did she know? Was this the mischief she had spoken of on their first encounter?

Eugenie turned to search for her dubious benefactor, as though the sight of her might confirm those suspicions. The firefly heart manifested a split-second before the full humanoid form. The fairy regarded her with a faint smile, her head tilted at a questioning angle.

Giving a fairy too much information was asking for trouble.

"I'm tired," said Eugenie, careful to keep her voice light. "You can take back your magic. I won't need it anymore tonight."

The smile broadened. "Of course." She flicked one dainty wrist. The gorgeous dress disintegrated from Eugenie's shoulders, replaced with her own worn clothing. Behind the fairy, the carriage evaporated into dust and swirled away on a whispering breeze.

A muffled thunk sounded in the night. Something glinted in the grass where the carriage had stood.

Eugenie's breath hitched. Stricken, she darted past the fairy to scoop up the fallen object. Her smoke-colored slipper reflected the moonlight, cold to the touch.

She raised wide, horrified eyes. The fairy watched her with the satisfaction of a well-fed cat. "I . . . I don't understand. Why didn't it disappear?"

The creature drew close, her canny expression alight. She spoke in all innocence, but her speech stabbed like a dagger to the heart. "Temporary magic can only have temporary consequences. If something permanent comes from it, a piece of the magic becomes permanent as well to keep the balance. What permanent consequence came of your attending the masquerade tonight, Eugenie of Pluterra?"

No answer would pass Eugenie's lips. She clutched the quartz shoe to her breast, her gaze unfocused as the evening's terrible revelation resurfaced.

It *couldn't* be—

"Did you already know?" she asked.

Feather-light fingers glanced off her shoulders as the ethereal creature swished past. "I'm your godmother, child. I know everything about you."

Godmother. The term had to mean something different to fairy-kind than to humans. But when had this creature ensnared her, and how? Her grip tightened around the slipper, her knuckles white. She redirected her thoughts.

"Only one shoe?" she asked, forcing herself to look up into the pointed face.

The fairy's smile dripped with indulgent sympathy. "There's no balance in only one shoe."

Despair escaped Eugenie's throat. She launched from the grass and bolted for the stairs. The fairy made no attempt to stop her or to call her back. She passed through the front door and slammed it shut, her back against it as though a horde of monsters chased her.

She couldn't breathe. The full weight of hopelessness crashed upon her. If everyone believed her dead, if Marielle owned this estate and everything within it, then Eugenie lived on her goodwill. She was a pauper, robbed of title, inheritance, and even her very existence.

But Marielle had always been so kind.

She forced an inhale as she slid to the floor. Eyes unfocused, she searched the shadowed ceiling for some remedy to this miserable ruin. Her whole world had turned upside-down, and the fairy's magic only deemed such a calamity equal to a pair of glittering shoes.

7
Unmasked

A CARRIAGE RATTLED UP the gravel to the front of the manor house. Eugenie, curled beneath a blanket next to the dying fire, listened as three bodies descended. The hackney drove away again as they tripped up the steps.

"I'm so tired!" Florelle declared, flouncing through the door.

"*You're* tired?" said Aurielle. "You spent half the night off in the corner flirting with Signore Falco, and it only ended up being our loathsome cousin, Edward Lavande. Your face at the unmasking, Florie! You were almost as horrified as he was!" Her peal of laughter echoed off the high ceilings in the entryway, followed by a cry of rage from her sister.

"Girls, please," Marielle said over the din. "You're both exhausted." Footsteps clacked across the tiled entryway. Eugenie, her back to the door, evened her breathing.

She couldn't face her stepmother. Not yet.

"Eugenie's asleep by the fire," said Marielle in a hush. "Hurry upstairs and get some rest yourselves."

Grumbling ensued. Florelle and Aurielle shoved one another back and forth as they mounted the staircase to the next floor.

Soot and Slipper

Marielle lingered. "Eugenie," she said, in a voice too forceful to ignore.

Feigning disorientation, Eugenie lifted her head. Her hair fell across her eyes, obscuring her view as she tilted her neck toward the doorway. "Hmm?"

"You left your shoes outside," said Marielle. She held aloft the pair of worn slippers. "They're soaked with dew."

"Sorry," Eugenie murmured, and she laid her head back down.

Her stepmother dropped the shoes within the room. She stayed for three breaths longer, as though she wished to ask something more, but then her footsteps retreated in a click-click-click across the entryway and up the stairs.

When three doors in the west wing had shut, Eugenie threw aside her blanket and sat up, miserable and restless. Two minutes passed with no further movement from the second floor. If last week was any indication, the Elles would sleep all morning and into the afternoon.

Like a ghost she drifted to the entryway, pausing only to slip her wet shoes on her feet. She pulled her threadbare cloak from its hook by the door and swung it around her shoulders. As she stepped outside, she tossed the hood up over her head.

Dawn had come, but a sheet of gray clouds blocked any view of the sun on the horizon and mist lumbered across the ground. The melancholy world mirrored her mood. She drew her cloak tight and walked quickly to the lane.

The cold morning seeped into her bones, the road deserted except for her own crunching footsteps. She paused when a farmer's wagon passed at a fork up ahead, obscured in the haze. It rumbled into the distance, the noise muffled around her. She shivered and continued onward, turning to follow its wake, toward the village of Hazelcross.

The cemetery lay beside the church, with the forest boundaries just beyond. She hadn't come as often as she should have, but she had never found comfort among stone pillars and memorial inscriptions. Her dying mother had begged her not to mourn. When her father put on a cheerful face to hide his grief, Eugenie could do nothing less.

Her own illness after his death, a rheumatic fever, had plagued her for the better part of a year. Even the short walk to the church was beyond her stamina for several months afterward. Marielle had long since sold the estate horses—an expense they could only keep by dipping into Eugenie's inheritance, she had claimed at the time. Eugenie had not returned to the cemetery more than once or twice since then.

And yet, according to Pip, the whole world believed she was a permanent resident there.

A misting rain began to fall as she crossed between the posts that marked the graveyard's boundaries. She passed a black carriage with a pair of equally black horses—some other early mourner—and threaded through gravestones to the stateliest set in the far corner. Her parents' monument, an edifice of white marble, glistened in the light rain. Ivy twisted up around its base, climbing toward the pair of names inscribed in the stone. It hugged her mother's death date, obscuring the last number in the year.

Marielle had planted it herself to symbolize the wedded love between her late husband and his first wife. Four years ago, Eugenie had thought it a sweet gesture.

Now, she ripped the encroaching tendrils back.

They left behind a layer of grime upon the whiteness. With ruthless efficiency she pulled them away to reveal the secret they hid beneath their climbing vines.

Soot and Slipper

Her own name met her gaze, *Eugenie Vivienne*, with a death date three years past.

Her breath rattled in her throat. The tears she could not cry during the night spilled down her cheeks as her numbness broke into despair.

It couldn't be. People couldn't possibly believe she was dead.

But she hadn't been to the village in ages. Her illness had thrown her into a pattern of confinement, and by the time her strength had built up enough to go, it was the younger Elles' job to fetch the groceries—"Their way of being useful," Marielle had said whenever Eugenie offered. "You wouldn't want to take that away from them, not when you already do so much here."

Cumbered by the burden of running the estate in Eugenie's name, Marielle had dismissed all but a single maid, Nanette, who had tended to Eugenie in the onset of her sickness. The maid had been her only companion after Marielle sent Florelle and Aurielle away to finishing school to avoid the disease.

But Nanette had not stayed even a month. Marielle said she was called home to her family.

Was that even true? Or had she dismissed her when she faked Eugenie's death?

The rainfall increased, though not to a full downpour. A cry of anguish wrenched from Eugenie's lips.

Was everything a lie? How could she have been so blind, so stupid?

"Excuse me," said someone to her left.

She jumped, startled, and set eyes upon a young man with a concerned expression beneath the hood of his dark cloak. He offered her a handkerchief. Reluctantly she took it, mortified to be discovered in such a fragile state. He stood beside her in awkward silence, his hands in his pockets as she wiped her tears away.

The handkerchief was too fine for her to blow her nose.

"Did you know the family well?" he asked, his voice tentative.

"Yes, intimately."

In the silence that followed, she chanced a look at his face. The jaw was too square to be Sir Pip, and his build was thicker too, though not by much. Relief flooded through her, that her benefactor was no one she might know. This was just another soul come to grieve. "I'm sorry I interrupted your mourning."

"Not at all," he said. He nodded toward her family's monument. "Do you need to talk about it?"

"No. I should be going." But where might she go? Could she return to her father's estate—an estate that Marielle owned outright, to which she had no legal claim? How could she even prove she was Eugenie of Pluterra and not some impostor?

This daunting thought overwhelmed her, knotting the pit of her stomach. She proffered the handkerchief back to her nameless companion, who received it with reluctance.

"Thank you," she said.

"Wait," he said when she turned to leave. She pretended not to hear, but quickened her step. "Wait! Cinderella!"

He caught her arm and spun her. She tore away in panic.

"How did you—? You're not him!" she cried, backing away from the young man. Guilt flashed across his face—an honest face, but not the correct one—as a clap of thunder announced a downpour. "You're not Pip! I know his voice, if nothing else!"

His lips parted, but he did not argue. Eugenie whirled, intent upon the cemetery exit. Tears flooded her eyes as betrayal snaked through her. Who but Pip knew that name?

She had not run more than five steps before a second figure blocked her path. She skidded to a halt, her pulse galloping in her throat.

Hands aloft to show he meant no harm, the newcomer said, "Cinderella, it's me."

The voice was right. And the jawline, and the shoulders, and everything about him except his missing smile.

No words escaped her lips. She glanced to the man behind her, who had backed away to the meager cover of some tall pine trees, and then to Sir Pip in front of her. Vaguely she registered the fineness of their clothing against her threadbare state, but her mental trauma dismissed any shallow mortification.

Who cared what she looked like?

"I'm sorry," Pip said, his expression earnest. "I thought you might come here, and I felt foolish coming by myself. My friend didn't mean you any harm. You left so suddenly last night, and I've been sick with worry ever since."

"I'm not dead," she said desperately.

Confusion pulled at his brows.

"I'm not dead." She flung an accusing finger back toward her family's monument. "I don't know how my name got on that stone, but I'm *not* dead."

Thunder pealed across the sky, and the storm redoubled.

"Eugenie of Pluterra," said Pip, as though staring at a ghost.

"I'm not dead!" she screamed and stamped her foot.

In two steps he closed the gap between them and enveloped her in a strong embrace. She dug her frozen fingers into his cloak and wailed against his shoulder, her heart a shattered vessel in her chest. He cradled her head and let her cry while the rain drenched them both.

His warmth and kindness lingered as her torrential outburst ebbed. Her sobs reduced to hiccups, and her mortification grew. When she pulled away, she lifted a tentative glance to his face.

He was the picture of sincerity and concern. "Let's get you

out of this storm," he said, and he tugged her along the path. She allowed him to lead her, until they came to the black carriage near the cemetery entrance. When Pip opened the door, she balked.

Marielle's warnings drummed in her ears. *A lady never enters a closed carriage with a man unescorted.*

"I can't—" The words caught in her throat.

Why should she listen to the counsel of a serpent? What kind of reputation did a dead person have to ruin?

With renewed determination, she climbed into the warm, dry interior. Pip, bemused and oblivious to her internal debate, followed and pulled the door shut.

"You're soaked to the bone," he said, making himself busy on the opposite seat. "Take off your cloak and wrap up in the blanket there. There's a hot brick underneath it. We'll get you warm again in no time."

The "blanket" was actually a coverlet, fur-lined and finer than anything Eugenie had ever seen. She hesitated but ultimately stripped her sodden cloak and wrapped up in the warm fur. A shiver traveled down her spine.

Across from her, Pip tossed a simpler woolen blanket around his own shoulders. His dark hair—brown, to match his eyes, and waving past his jaw—had a light sheen of rain on it. Silence settled between them, charged with a hundred unspoken questions. Who was he, and why would he help her? Was he the master of this carriage and its finery, or had he drawn upon his friend's resources?

Their acquaintance amounted to a few paltry hours together, but somehow he was her only ally in the world.

What must he think, to find his masquerade partner in such a shabby state?

Soot and Slipper

The carriage door abruptly opened. Eugenie stifled a shriek. "Where am I driving this trap?" asked Pip's nameless friend, carefully not glancing in her direction.

Pip looked to Eugenie. "Is there an inn in the village? You'd do well with a fire right now."

She tensed. "I shouldn't—"

"You're *not* dead, and I'd prefer we kept it that way."

His fervid expression banished her misgivings. If she caught a fatal illness now, only a pauper's grave awaited her. She eased back into her seat. "The Gray Goose," she said, listless. "It's on the main road, on the other side of the village."

"I think I saw it coming in," said the friend, and he shut the door. The carriage jostled as he climbed onto the driver's box. When it lurched into motion, Eugenie's nerves bubbled over.

She leaned forward, babbling. "I don't have any money. I only came down from the manor house to check whether it was true. I didn't really believe—" Her voice caught on a sob.

He settled his palm on her clasped hands, his touch like a jolt of lightning up her arms. "Don't worry about a thing. We'll get everything back into its proper frame, I promise you."

But sick despair had already taken root in her soul. "How can you promise any such thing? If everyone believes I'm dead, how can I prove I'm Eugenie of Pluterra and not some charlatan?"

He blinked. "Aren't there any servants at the house who can vouch for your identity?"

She shook her head, her vision blurred with tears. "She turned them all off years ago. She said she couldn't justify dipping into my inheritance for her comforts, but that if I wanted a maid for myself that was my right. But how could I allow someone to wait upon me when she and the younger Elles refused to have the courtesy extended to them?"

"The people in your village—"

"I haven't been there in *years*, Pip."

A disbelieving laugh fluttered from his throat. "Why not?"

"Because I was sick, and the recovery was so long that—Oh, I *know* it's preposterous. I *am* Eugenie! But how am I to prove it?"

He muddled over the conundrum, his gaze unfocused. When he spoke, it was barely above a whisper. "The prince will vouch for you. You said you met him as a child."

"We're not children anymore. Why should he remember me?"

His brown eyes lifted to examine her, his gaze so intense that it took her breath away. "He will. You're far too charming to forget."

Had she met Pip before? Did he have some clout with the royal family, that he could ensure their cooperation on her behalf?

He cupped her hands in his as he studied her face. "Where did you meet him?"

Eugenie swallowed. The memory surfaced, bitter and sweet wrapped together. "He came to my mother's funeral. His parents forced him, I think. We were the only children there, and I was trying so hard to be strong—for my mother and father both." Glimpses of that somber morning flashed through her mind's eye: the dark coffin, the sonorous priest, the smell of pine boughs that had warded off the encroaching scent of death. She suppressed a shudder and continued her tale. "When the service ended, after I pitched my handful of dirt into the grave, the prince caught me by the wrist and pulled me into the forest while no one was looking. 'You can cry all you want here,' he said. Then he stood guard over me, and I cried until my heart was wrung dry."

Her eyes brimmed with tears as she raised them to meet Pip's gaze. "There's no reason for him to remember that. It was only a small kindness on his part. His parents must have taken him to dozens of funerals."

He digested the story, his expression unreadable. "Did you get in trouble for running off?"

"Not me. His mother scolded him when they finally found us, though."

A smile cracked across his face, and he squeezed her hands. "Then maybe she'll remember."

Eugenie huffed a rueful laugh.

"Did you never see him again?" he asked.

She looked to the window, to the rain streaming down the glass. It rendered the passing homes of Hazelcross into a blur. "I never spoke with him again, not face to face. There were..." Her fleeting glance darted toward Pip, who was intent upon her every word. A wry smile tipped her mouth. "Don't think too much of this. He wrote me in the months that followed, just short letters to ask how I was doing, and I responded with equal politeness."

"And you think he wouldn't remember you?" Pip asked, brows arched.

"I think he wrote dozens of those letters, to people all over the country. It was a formality, complete with his full title and the whole string of names—he has six or seven of them, you know. His Royal Highness Louis Fernand Renaud Theophilus something-or-other. And I only had two to sign in return."

The carriage stopped in the inn yard. Outside, Pip's friend hopped to the gravel and ran for the sheltered entrance.

"Long names are a hallowed tradition among our noble class," said Pip with a careless wave. He peered through the downpour to the retreating figure and spoke as though nonchalant. "They ward off fairy curses, because fairies can't be bothered to memorize more than three in a string. I'm surprised your parents let you get away with only two."

Perhaps that was the instrument her "godmother" had used to claim her. Eugenie twiddled the fur lining of her blanket, loath to broach the topic of fairies along with everything else. "Anyway, the correspondence stopped after my father and Marielle got married. It had to, unless the prince wanted to write Florelle and Aurielle too. He did come to the wedding with his parents, but they were across the church from where I sat. Marielle sent me and her girls home as soon as the ceremony finished, so we wouldn't have to wait while everyone greeted them."

A muscle rippled along Pip's jaw. "That's a shame," he said, his gaze still fixed out the window. "Still, I think he has every reason in the world to remember you."

Although he spoke with gravity, she could not agree. A decade had passed since that time. And she had, apparently, been dead for three of those years.

The friend returned, his arms raised above his head to ward off the pelting rain. "I've let a private parlor," he said, and he motioned for them to hurry inside. They ran through the deluge. At the door, the innkeeper's wife gawked at Eugenie's fur wrapping as she gestured them into the cozy interior. She barely glanced at the pair of men.

The private parlor was small but warm. "Sit over here by the fire," Pip said, drawing an armchair close for her to curl up in. Seeing her thus ensconced, he crossed to the door, where he exchanged words with his friend in a voice too low for Eugenie to overhear. The friend left, and Pip returned to drape his wet cloak and hers over two more chairs by the hearth.

She watched him in silence, her head against the padded armrest. He worked with care in movements precise and efficient.

Even without his half-mask and dark cloak, he yet presented a mystery.

"Who are you?" she asked. "Why are you being so nice to me?"

"Why shouldn't I be nice to you?" he replied, wringing the water from his cloak's hem onto the floor.

She sat up on an elbow. "There's no benefit to you."

He spread the cloak again on its chair and positioned it closer to the fire. Favoring her with an earnest smile, he said, "Benefit? It's penance, more like. You provided me with the very best of company on *two* occasions, and I repaid your kindness by telling you that you were dead. Not all the niceness in the world can make up for such an offense." His eyes twinkled, but contrition lurked in their depths.

She had no stomach for jokes, however well-intentioned they were. "Where did your friend go?"

"He's asking around the village to see what people know about the manor house and who lives there." His expression turned intent. "You've really been in seclusion all these years?"

"I was ill," she said, curling up again on the armrest. "Marielle even sent her girls away so they wouldn't catch it. It's a wonder I didn't die. Or maybe I did, and I'm a ghost who can't accept her fate. Maybe I have to perform some service to move on to the afterlife."

Pip crouched in front of her. "You're not a ghost," he said, and he gently brushed a strand of bedraggled hair from her face. When she made a noise of discontent, he caught her hand, never breaking eye contact. "You're flesh and blood, Cinderella."

Warmth traveled up her arms and spread into her very bones. A chilling thought chased it away. "Who's buried with my parents, then? Or was it an empty box they put in the grave?"

"There was no box," he said.

Her heart stuttered. "What?"

"You died—*she* died—" He shook his head, flustered, and tried again. "It happened during an outbreak of influenza. There were so many deaths across the country that the coffin-makers couldn't keep up with the demand, so the crown decreed that all burials—noble and peasant alike—had to be in a shroud alone. There's a body in that grave, but it was only wrapped in black linen."

Her disbelief magnified into horror. If this was true, it meant that Marielle had gotten a corpse somewhere, had passed it off as her stepdaughter and staged a funeral to show the world that she was dead. The House of Pluterra had met its end in a macabre charade.

A shiver pulsed through her. She gripped his hand as though it were her only connection to the truth. "What am I to do, Sir Pip?"

He laid a warm, comforting palm upon her head. "Sleep for now. I'll wake you in a couple of hours."

How could he suggest sleep when her mind was aflame? But she rested her head back anyway. The fire crackled, and Pip paced to the opposite side of the room, to a writing desk. Soon enough, the scratch of a nib against paper met her ears. As she stared at the dark crossbeams on the ceiling, her harrowed night caught up to her. Her eyelids drooped, and she drifted from consciousness, half-anxious and half-satisfied that Marielle would disapprove her sleeping there.

8
Vale of Gloom

"You're crazy, Nic. Crazy. Everyone in the village says—"

"I don't care what everyone says. I know who she is."

The argument, though hushed, rose in volume enough to pull Eugenie from her slumber. She opened her eyes to a crackling fire in the grate. Nestled within the fur-lined coverlet, she held perfectly still, her breath in her throat as she listened.

"You're talking about deceit of the very worst kind," said Pip's friend. "If you don't have solid proof to back your claims—"

"The solid proof is curled up in that chair," Pip replied.

Eugenie, dread pooling within her, lifted her head. She met the friend's gaze, but he averted his attention to the hallway.

Pip, who had flung one finger to point at her, did a double take. He abandoned the argument and hurried to her side. "Are you all right?"

"What's happened?" she asked, sitting up. She rubbed grit from the corners of her eyes. "What time is it?"

"Noon. We're having lunch brought in shortly. Can you eat something?"

She shook her head, her appetite nonexistent. Instead she peered to his friend, who lingered by the door with misgivings plain upon him. "What did the villagers say?"

"It's not important," said Pip.

A rebellious spark lit her countenance. "Of course it is."

He sat back on his heels. With resignation, he beckoned his friend to join them. "Go on. Tell her."

The friend perched on the edge of the nearest chair. His conviction of only moments before had fled. With utmost politeness, he asked, "Who is Nanette, my lady?"

A leaden weight settled in her chest. "She was our maid. She left us three years ago, about a month after my illness set in. Marielle said she went home to her family, that they needed her help more than we did."

"You see?" Pip said, but his friend only shook his head.

It wasn't difficult to guess the source of their disagreement. Eugenie spoke her conclusion aloud, her voice dull. "Everyone in the village thinks I'm Nanette."

"We'll sort it out," said Pip.

The friend jostled him with a foot to the back, but his contrition returned as he addressed Eugenie. "Everyone I spoke with said that Baroness Lavande and her two daughters live with only a maid to tend them—Nanette, who comes from a village somewhere east of here."

"A village that Theo's about to set off in search of," said Pip.

His friend scowled.

Eugenie, more hopeless than ever despite her rest, settled back in her chair. "Is that your name? Theo?" The friend, flustered, ducked his head in acknowledgement. Eugenie toyed with her fingertips. "And you think I'm Nanette too."

"I don't—"

"He doesn't know what he thinks," Pip interjected.

"Nic, be serious," said Theo.

"Nic?" Eugenie asked before they could erupt into another argument. "Short for Nicolas?"

"Dominic," Pip said. He favored her with a rueful smile. "And now you know the extent of my imagination: Dominic the Domino."

Behind him, Theo snorted and muttered under his breath, "If only."

Pip swatted his legs. "If it's all the same, Milady, I'm happy for you to continue calling me Sir Pip."

"I think we're past the point of masquerading," she said.

Theo snorted again and received another swat for his troubles.

"You," said Pip in rebuke. "If you're so convinced she's not who she says she is, get a horse from the hostler and track down this village to the east."

"Leaving you to drive the carriage, I suppose," said Theo with a bite of sarcasm.

"We both know I'm perfectly capable."

Eugenie watched the interchange, unable to determine their relationship. Were they master and servant? But Theo didn't look like any servant she had ever seen, and Pip treated him more like a brother or a close friend, even if he did order him around.

And yet, Theo seemed the elder of the pair, so he should have ordered Pip around if they had equal standing.

"You're crazy," said Theo, confirmation that he was no servant. "You'd send me off in this kind of weather, with hardly a lead to follow? It's a wild goose chase."

"If you won't believe Eugenie or me, then you deserve it," said Pip, leaning back on his elbows as though he had not a concern in the world. "Go find your proof that she's Nanette."

Theo glanced self-consciously toward Eugenie. "It's not that I don't believe you," he said apologetically. "It's just . . . I was at her funeral. We all were. Practically the whole country saw her body lowered into the earth. By the time we'd all cast in our handful of dirt, the gravediggers had hardly any work left to do. The whole of Jacondria believes that Eugenie of Pluterra is dead and buried."

Her eyes slid shut, his words a knell upon her soul.

"Get your horse and go," said Pip, more irritated than angry.

Theo kept his chair. "Think what this means, Nic. You're saying that Baroness Lavande faked her stepdaughter's death and stole her inheritance."

"Yes," Pip said on a hiss.

"You've never liked her, not since—"

"Never mind that."

"But it makes no sense. Why would she then allow the same stepdaughter to come to the royal masquerades and move among the nobles who believe her dead?"

"She made her leave again before the unmasking," said Pip.

"She didn't let me go at all," said Eugenie. She opened her eyes to the pair's confused gazes upon her. The leaden weight on her heart intensified. She gathered the fur coverlet almost to her chin, huddling in its softness.

"What—" Pip began.

"She asked me not to go. She wants Florelle and Aurielle to find husbands and said I might be a distraction for any of their prospective suitors."

"I'll say," Theo muttered, eyeing her from top to bottom. Whatever else he disapproved, it wasn't her looks—at least not in comparison with her stepsisters.

Eugenie flushed crimson and continued as though he hadn't spoken. "I agreed to stay home. But then I didn't."

"So who was your benefactor?" asked Pip. "Was it the same seamstress who made their costumes? The one they refuse to disclose to anyone?"

She slouched a fraction deeper into her chair. "I made their costumes."

"*You*?" said Theo. His expression twisted. "If you're a nobleman's daughter, how could you possibly know how to sew like a tradeswoman?"

Her eyes flashed. "Spend weeks in a sickbed and you'll learn just about anything to relieve the boredom. I started taking dresses apart at the seams and piecing them back together again. It's not hard once you know how everything fits."

"So you made your own costumes," Pip said, though bewilderment still hovered around him.

"No." Eugenie averted her attention to the window, where a thread of cold air seeped in from the gray daylight beyond.

"Then who—?"

"What happened to my slipper?" she asked, fiddling with her blanket. "Do you have it with you? I'm going to need it back."

"I don't have it," he said.

Her gaze snapped to his face, her breath tight in her lungs. "Where is it?"

He opened his mouth as though to make excuses, but his expression turned apologetic. "With the queen. She saw it in my hands when I returned to the masquerade, and she asked me for it."

Dread plunged through Eugenie like a vat of ice water. Blood drained from her cheeks and an odd light-headedness warned her against any sudden movement.

Fairy mischief, indeed.

"Who is your benefactor?" Pip asked.

"My godmother," she said in a listless voice.

He sat up straight. "You have a godmother? Then *she* can vouch for who you are."

A cynical noise escaped her throat. "But no one would believe her. Even I wouldn't." Confusion descended on Pip and Theo both. Eugenie, determined to have everything out in the open at last, leaned forward, interlacing her fingers and wringing them. "I don't have a godmother, not really. It was a fairy. She showed up in the garden after the Elles left for the masquerade last week, and she said if I returned before midnight that none of the magic would cause any permanent consequences."

Pip's grave expression mirrored on Theo's face. Perhaps they were brothers, or cousins. A fluttering, half-desperate laugh tumbled from Eugenie's lips. She tossed her hands up in defeat. "I just wanted to go to a party. We were living in poverty and it was my fault, because Marielle refused to touch my inheritance for her own comforts—or so she always said." Her words choked on a sob. She looked to the wall, willing the emotion away.

"You bargained with a fairy?" Theo asked. "So you're fairy-cursed now on top of everything else?"

Eugenie shook her head. "The fairy said she couldn't curse me. She already knew my name, and she swore the magic was only temporary. And it was, the first time. The shoes remained behind last night because I learned that everyone thinks I'm dead—a permanent consequence instead of a temporary one. And I think . . . I think that's the whole reason the fairy wanted me to go." She locked gazes with Pip, who wore an unreadable expression. Her voice turned piteous. "You do believe me, don't you?"

A tense moment passed. Would he deny her? Declaim anything to do with her, all because of a fairy's mischievous intervention?

But when he finally spoke, he said nothing of the fairy at all. "You have the other shoe?"

She nodded, bemused.

"Good." He pushed from the floor, his manner brusque. "Theo, get a horse from the hostler."

"But—"

"*Now*."

Any fight vanished on that iron command. Theo hefted from his chair and ushered out the door without another word. Pip, in his absence, paced to the writing desk and back, his movement swift.

The fairy's involvement changed everything. It undermined her whole story: fairies could alter a person's looks, or their memories. Anyone who dealt with fairies became unreliable and untrustworthy in the aftermath. Eugenie, conscious of her mistake, pushed the coverlet aside and slowly stood.

Pip paused halfway across the room, an inquiry in his eyes.

She plucked up her cloak, mostly dry now, from where it hung near the fire. "I think it's time for me to go home," she said in little better than a whisper. "They'll wake up soon if they haven't already." But when she stepped toward the door, he blocked her path.

"You can't go back there."

A harrowed little laugh escaped her throat. "Then where am I to go? The only place I have in this world is as a servant in my own house."

He grasped her arms below the shoulders and looked her square in the eyes. "Eugenie, there's a body in your grave. We don't know how that person died, whether it was natural causes or whether—" His voice cut out before he could pronounce the fatal accusation.

Anxiety laced her ribcage tighter than a corset. "Marielle wouldn't kill someone." Even as the words left her mouth, she second-guessed them. Her stepmother had always acted cordially to her, but there was an underlying ruthlessness about her that unsettled Eugenie.

Pip's somber demeanor in no way allayed her fears. "How do you know that? She convinced the whole country that you're dead. Do you think she expects to keep you hidden on that estate forever?"

What did Marielle mean to do with her? How would she keep up the charade when Eugenie became old enough to claim her inheritance? How would she react if Eugenie insisted on going to the next masquerade, or if she asked to be presented at court? Nothing made sense anymore.

She shook the troubling questions away, but her panic escalated nonetheless. "If she intended to kill me, she might have done it any time these past three years. Why would she let me live if she were such a villain?"

His grip upon her arms tensed. "I don't know. But I can't let you go back there."

"I have *nowhere else to go*, Pip. She doesn't know that I know. If I get home before she wakes up, she won't even suspect. And maybe the best thing to do would be to ask her outright—"

"You can't *confront* her. You don't know what she's capable of."

Eugenie favored him with a skeptical frown. "She's barely a dab of a thing. And if she has such terrible plans for me, what do you think she'll do if I suddenly disappear?"

He blinked, his gaze unfocused as he digested this question. Eugenie stooped to catch his attention again. Her voice dropped to a near-whisper.

"Theo said you never liked her. Why?"

Soot and Slipper

Pip's mouth pulled to one side. He averted his gaze. "It's nothing. I don't care what she does if she finds you gone. If you go back to that house, I—"

But he didn't complete the sentence. His hands trembled on her shoulders and he looked so torn that Eugenie didn't know what to think.

"Why have you never liked Marielle?" she quietly asked.

"She's a gold-digger," he said, flint in his words and his gaze fixed upon the wall. "She married for a title and fortune, wasted her first husband's estate, and then married your father for another fortune—*and* she staged your death when your father left her nothing more than a pittance. Why should I like her? Eugenie, as your *friend*, as someone who cares deeply that you remain safe in this world, I beg you not to return to that house."

"And where do you propose I go instead?" She peered up at him, wondering how he might respond. Was he willing to offer his protection, and could she even accept such a thing if he did?

But the offer didn't come.

"Go to the queen," he said. "Plead your case. She can reinstate your family title and give you protection."

"And how do I prove to her who I am?" Even as he opened his mouth to respond, she added, "And don't tell me to rely on the prince. He might believe, as Theo does, that I'm an impostor."

"He'll vouch for you," said Pip, a stubborn set to his mouth. "I swear to you he will."

He couldn't swear any such thing with assurance, but Eugenie recognized when someone was past reasoning. "Any proof of who I am lies in that manor house, Pip," she said, and she gently skirted from his grasp. "The family portrait from when I was a child, my sketchbooks and my diary..." Even her letters from the prince, if those could serve as evidence, she had squirreled away in a packet beneath her bed so the Elles would never find them.

"And the fairy shoe?" he asked, his gaze distant again.

She nodded. She'd hidden it last night after bolting into the house.

Indecision warred upon his face. At long last he gripped her hands and locked eyes with her. His intensity pierced her to her core. "Swear to me that you won't confront her."

Eugenie hesitated. "I—"

"Please, I beg of you. I won't have a moment's peace until you're free of that house, of that woman. Swear you won't confront her."

"All right. I swear." It was more for his sake than hers. She couldn't imagine her stepmother physically lashing out against anyone. Marielle's words could be sharp, cutting, but she had never resorted to physical violence.

Except, perhaps, against the unknown body in Eugenie's grave...

The vow elicited a breath of relief from Pip. He swallowed and regrouped himself. "Go through the rest of your day as though it were any other. Don't act suspicious, don't gather your things. I have an idea, but it might take time to orchestrate. Will you meet me tonight so I know nothing has happened to you?"

Her brows arched. "Meet you where?"

"Isn't there a garden or something on the estate?"

"It's right next to the house. The Elles would be able to see you out the windows."

"I'll keep to the bushes. Make an excuse to take a walk at dusk. I'll tell you my plans then."

It seemed a simple enough request. When she agreed, he pressed her hands, his eyes bright.

He drove her home, too, almost to the manor house. The carriage stopped in a bend just out of sight from the estate, and Pip hopped from the driver's box to open her door. The swath of gray overhead still spit an occasional raindrop, but it was nothing to the morning's downpour.

"Remember: act natural," Pip said as he handed her to the ground, though he looked like he would sooner bundle her back into the carriage than let her go.

On impulse, she pressed her palm to his cheek. "It's all right." She sounded more confident than she felt. Everything since last night's masquerade played upon her thoughts like a nightmare. Perhaps she would wake up in her own bed soon. Or perhaps she could divine the truth of Marielle's treachery. She would certainly learn nothing by running away.

He kissed her fingers and withdrew, his hands in fists at his side and his eyes fixed upon her. Eugenie felt his gaze every step of her retreat. When she reached the curve that would take her beyond his sight, she paused to raise her hand in one last farewell.

He returned the gesture, somber though his expression was. And yet, the mere fact that he waited at all warmed her soul. After a deep breath to boost her confidence, she continued up the road and past the fence posts that marked the estate boundaries. She listened for sounds of a retreating carriage, but they did not come until she was almost to the house, the clatter hardly more than a whisper carried along the road.

9
Suspicion Ignited

THE MANOR HOUSE was quiet. Eugenie slipped inside and set her shoes and her cloak by the door. Her pulse thundered in her throat. Every inch past the fence posts had increased her paranoia, but surely she was in no danger here.

"Out for a walk?"

She started, barely stifling a shriek, and spun to find her stepmother at the top of the stairs. Marielle looked down at her with a question on her pretty face.

Act natural.

"Yes," Eugenie said, her hand at her heart.

The woman descended like a queen, one hand upon the balustrade. The poise that Eugenie had always admired twisted from refinement into a sign of dominance. The fingers upon the wooden railing claimed ownership. Every step was the step of a master in her own house.

"You didn't walk far, I hope," Marielle said, a note of concern in her voice, "especially on a gray day like this. You know how delicate your health is."

"Yes. I mean—I didn't walk far." Realizing that her stepmother may have seen her coming from the lane, she added, "I only went a little up the road."

"And did you get rained on?"

Eugenie shrank from the woman's piercing scrutiny and lied again. "Not very much."

Marielle made an exasperated noise. "You *know* how dangerous it is for you to overexert yourself, and getting caught in a rainstorm is only going to make the stress on your body that much worse."

This was a pattern Eugenie could easily navigate. Marielle fussed about her health on almost a daily basis. She'd always assumed it was her stepmother's way of showing concern.

"I'm all right. I just needed some time outside. I've been in my workroom so much these past two weeks."

"That's my fault, I suppose," said Marielle, rounding the newel post on her way toward the kitchen. She paused when she spied Eugenie's tattered slippers by the door. "I never did ask: how did you manage to leave your shoes outside last night?"

Eugenie glanced to the footwear with a self-conscious swallow. "I went for a walk in the garden after you left and . . . uh . . . got too close to the pond, I guess. My shoes were soaked, so I left them outside, but then I forgot to bring them in."

Her stepmother tipped her head in voiceless rebuke.

"I'm sorry." The apology slipped breathless from Eugenie's lips.

Marielle brushed it aside. "It's no harm to *me* if you leave your shoes out in the cold and wet. But we should probably get you some new ones anyway. The bottoms of those are almost worn through, and the toes have completely lost their finish."

"I don't really go anywhere," Eugenie said, as she always did when her stepmother mentioned the state of her footwear.

Marielle usually responded with an epithet—"You sweet child," or some such endearment—but this time she only hummed.

The flat sound spiked Eugenie's heart rate. "How was the masquerade last night?" she asked to change the subject.

Marielle started to answer, but the sound of a door upstairs interrupted her. Above, Florelle trudged into view with a wide yawn. Another door opened and shut, and Aurielle appeared behind her sister, almost bouncing with energy.

"The girls had two of the most beautiful costumes of the night," said Marielle as her daughters descended.

Aurielle passed her sister halfway down. "I was the only ruby," she announced with smug triumph. "Florie had half a dozen roses to compete with."

"But mine was the best," Florelle said, jostling her sister in the back. Aurielle stumbled the last two steps but caught herself on the railing before she hit the tile. She turned venomous eyes upon Florelle, who ignored her in favor of fixating on Eugenie. "Still, you could have come up with something more original for me. And Mother's raven almost blended into the crowd."

Eugenie's attention snapped to Marielle, who only shrugged aside the assertion, though her eyes sparked with annoyance. "There were a lot of black costumes this time, but I don't need to stand out. Florelle and Aurielle both had no dearth of admirers."

A snigger erupted from Aurielle. Florelle launched at her throat with an indignant squeal. Eugenie edged toward the back hallway as Marielle pulled the sisters apart.

"Honestly, girls, behave yourselves. Aurielle, stop needling your sister. It may have just as easily been you who spent the night flirting with your cousin. Eugenie."

The sound of her own name stopped Eugenie from skirting out of sight. She froze, eyes wide upon the trio.

"Where are you going?" Marielle asked while her daughters signaled threats at each other behind her back.

Eugenie vaguely gestured toward the hall. "To... to my workroom?"

"Have you eaten?"

She hadn't. Even the normality of the younger Elles' fight couldn't settle her strained nerves. She might retch if she had to eat anything.

Marielle sighed her disapproval. "Come to the kitchen with us. You have to keep your strength up." She dragged her daughters behind her the opposite direction.

Eugenie, with one wistful glance toward her failed escape route, followed. She had promised Pip she would act natural. Any day before this, she would have followed her stepfamily without fear, tickled that they had remembered to invite her.

Florelle and Aurielle flopped into chairs at the small table. Eugenie, at the door, tensed when Marielle pulled a knife from the drawer.

Her stepmother withdrew the stale half-loaf of bread that remained, but she paused before cutting. "Did you eat last night?" she asked, studying the loaf.

"Yes," said Eugenie.

Marielle lifted a narrowed gaze. "What did you have?"

Standing there with her critical stare and a long, serrated knife held upright, she looked like a would-be murderer about to launch into her crime.

Or perhaps Eugenie's imagination was running rampant. "I had an egg," she said.

Marielle glance toward the basket on the opposite countertop, unable to judge whether its contents had changed from yesterday to today. "That's all?"

Eugenie shrugged. "I had a handful of grapes, too."

Again Marielle couldn't verify whether that comestible had reduced in quantity. Her jaw tightened. She returned her attention to sawing through the loaf. "This bread is stale. We'll have to toast it. Eugenie, you know best what you're doing."

The remark spurred her from her place next to the door. She hopped across the room, hyper-aware of the knife in her stepmother's hand even as she pretended not to notice it. Florelle and Aurielle lolled on the table, happy to let others prepare their food. Marielle joined them when Eugenie took over.

Buttered toast and three-minute eggs soon graced the table, along with the last of their grapes, the vines withered and the fruit puckering where it attached at the stems.

Florelle sucked on one dusky globule and spat the seeds on the floor. "I want to go as a sunset next week," she said.

Aurielle, in the midst of spoon-cracking her egg, jolted upright. "Then *I* want to be a sunrise."

Her sister bristled, but before she could launch into an argument, Marielle interjected. "I think, perhaps, we should skip this week and let Eugenie rest. Can't you see how tired she is?"

As three pairs of eyes shifted to Eugenie, she instinctively cut stiff. "I'm not—"

"You fell asleep amid the ashes last night," said Marielle, "like a commoner living in a hut. I've told you not to sleep so near the fire, but I recognize it's our fault. We've run you ragged these past two weeks. You deserve a break."

She punctuated this statement with a kindly smile, but it had the opposite of its intended effect. Eugenie, dread churning her insides, lowered her gaze to her plate. Did her stepmother suspect...? Was this a ploy to keep Eugenie under tighter control? "Thank you," she said quietly.

Soot and Slipper

Florelle and Aurielle seethed for the rest of the silent meal.

As the first to finish, Eugenie gathered up her dishes and pushed back from the table.

"What are your plans for this afternoon?" Marielle abruptly asked.

"I—" She glanced from her stepmother to her stepsisters. "I thought I would start more costumes. Even if you skip this week, it doesn't hurt for me to sketch ideas now rather than later."

Florelle immediately perked. "A sunset!" she cried. "And don't make Aurielle a sunrise, or anything else that could be better than mine!"

Her sister shrieked. "Why should you get a better costume than me?"

"Because yours has been better two weeks in a row, you self-important parsnip! It's *my* turn to shine!"

"Girls!" Marielle thundered, her voice harsh enough to stop a tavern brawl. Her daughters froze, eyes huge upon her. She, however, looked to Eugenie. Tightly she said, "I really would rather you rest. I insist, in fact."

Eugenie vaguely nodded.

"As for you two, we need bread and some other groceries, unless you'd rather starve this week. Whose turn is it to run to the village?"

"Aurie's," said Florelle at the same time that Aurielle said, "Florie's."

They looked to one another like conspirators betrayed. "I went last week," Aurielle said in utmost rage.

"You did not. I did."

"You liar!"

"You lazy dog!"

Aurielle's outraged gasp could have punctured an eardrum.

Eugenie, belatedly recalling that she was supposed to act as she normally would, said, "I can go."

Again the room froze. Florelle swatted Aurielle as though to prod her out the door.

"You need to rest," said Marielle in tones that brooked no argument. "Florelle, Aurielle, if you can't agree on who went last week, then perhaps you should both go together."

They swallowed their disputes and quickly left the kitchen. Eugenie, taut with the terror of being alone with her stepmother, followed in their wake. She detoured to her workroom only to collect her sketchbook—something she deemed her unenlightened self would have done—and then retreated to her bedroom on the opposite side of the house from where the Elles lived.

She passed a tense afternoon drafting costume ideas—sunsets, myrtle trees, dragonflies—all while keeping one eye on her bedroom door, wary of what might lurk on the other side.

10
Tinderbox

AFTERNOON SHADOWS STRETCHED across Eugenie's room when the front door of the manor house slammed. A bloodcurdling yell echoed through the halls. Heart in her throat, she scrambled from her bed and tore from her room. The yell devolved into wails punctuated with stamping feet. Eugenie emerged onto the second-floor landing as her stepmother appeared from downstairs.

Florelle, in the midst of a shrieking tantrum in the entryway, acknowledged neither of them.

"What on earth has happened?" Marielle asked, a rebuke in her severe voice.

But Florelle only sank to the floor on a frenzied sob.

Aurielle lingered by the front door with the grocery basket perched on one hip and a malicious smile on her lips. "A royal crier came through the village while we were there with a proclamation from the queen," she said. "The prince has fallen in love."

"He has *not*," Florelle screeched. "He only saw that overdressed strumpet from afar! He's not in love with her!" She beat her fists against the tile, only stopping when her mother seized her wrists.

"Calm yourself this instant," said Marielle in deathly tones. Florelle blanched and shut her mouth. In the stifling hush that followed, the baroness shifted her focus to her other daughter. "Explain."

No impish smile dared manifest on Aurielle's face now. She shifted the basket into both hands, almost as a shield between her and her mother. "It's as I said. The crier came through. The prince has fallen in love with that masquerader, the Queen of the Night—or Milady Flame, as she last appeared."

At the top of the stairs, Eugenie gripped the handrail.

Aurielle continued. "She lost one of her slippers when she left, and the queen has commanded for her to come to court tomorrow, to claim her shoe and Prince Fernand's heart."

Florelle mewled an impotent protest.

"I don't know why you're so upset, Florie," said Aurielle in callous observation. "He never would've chosen someone with a face like yours."

Her mother's grasp on her prevented Florelle from scratching her sister's eyes out.

"Has he seen the face of this masquerader, then?" Marielle asked.

"No," said Florelle in a snarl. "He never went anywhere near her. She only danced with that wretched domino again and then disappeared before half the guests had arrived. But you remember how all those men fawned upon her? And now she's snared the prince as well!"

Her mother remained unmoved to her theatrical anguish. "If he hasn't seen her face, how will he know her when she comes to claim her shoe?"

"She has to try it on and show everyone that it fits," said Aurielle.

"And do you really think there's only one foot that fits into that shoe?"

Silence possessed the younger Elles. Their mother released her hold on Florelle's wrists and straightened, primly brushing the wrinkles from her skirt. "Really, girls, I expected more from you. If the prince hasn't seen the masquerader's face, then the shoe and his heart are anyone's to claim."

Florelle sniffed and wiped her runny nose with the back of her hand. "But," she said, her voice thick, "everyone knows it's not us. We all took off our masks at the end of the night, and everyone knows what costumes we wore."

"But do they know whether you wore the same costume all night long?" asked Marielle, her voice light. "There were too many people to keep track of everyone there. Masquerades invite this kind of mischief, switching looks to cause confusion. Who's to say that this mystery girl didn't disappear early and return wearing something else? Who can say that she wasn't a rose or a ruby?"

"But if she comes to claim the shoe herself..." said Florelle, faintly aghast at what her mother was proposing.

Marielle waved aside the concern. "That seems unlikely. If she wanted to engage the prince's affection, she'd have flirted with him outright. It's far more probable that she and this domino of hers are already attached—perhaps they're already married, even. In that case, she would have no cause to claim a prince or a shoe she so carelessly left behind. Or perhaps some misfortune befell her, and she can't return to stake her claim. Regardless, even if she does show up, if someone else fits the shoe before her, why shouldn't they claim the prize that comes with it?"

Guarded hope burned within Florelle's eyes. "You mean—?"

"If you want your prince so badly," said her mother, "we'll go to court ourselves and you can shove your foot into that shoe however you please."

Aurielle took a stilted step forward, bristling. "What about me?"

"What about you?" Marielle replied. "No one's stopping you from trying it on as well. You're neither of you going to win anything on your looks, so you need to take advantage of whatever opportunity presents itself."

At the top of the stairs, Eugenie fought the urge to protest. Her stepmother's assessment—that the true owner of the shoe likely had no inclination to claim it—was true, but to hoodwink the queen or the prince? She could not stomach the thought. If the ruse succeeded, the Elles would cheat their way into the highest echelons of society.

Just like they had cheated Eugenie out of her inheritance.

Florelle eagerly scrambled off the floor. "I'll wear my lavender gown, with my pearl necklace and flowers in my hair."

"You'd better hope that shoe is the size of a boat if you want to fit your paddles in there," said Aurielle.

"Like yours are any smaller," Florelle shot back. "I'll fit my foot in one way or another. It'll be fine unless that girl has freakishly dainty feet like Mama or Eugenie."

As though mere mention of her name awakened them to her presence, the Elles turned to view her at the top of the stairs. Eugenie, yet frozen in place, forced an anemic smile. "Is everything all right?" she asked, her voice small.

"After tomorrow, everything will be perfect," Florelle announced, and she paraded up the stairs en route to her bedroom.

Aurielle, yet in possession of their basket of groceries, plumped her lower lip in a pout.

Marielle simply shook her head and confiscated the goods. "Upstairs to your wardrobe," she said. "Whether you or your sister is the next queen, plan on looking your best." She followed the line of her daughters' retreat, but her attention shifted to Eugenie. A faint smile tipped up one corner of her mouth. "Fortune sometimes presents interesting opportunities. If all goes in our favor, you won't be burdened with our presence for much longer."

"I'm not—" Eugenie started, but the rest of the sentence caught in her throat. Beneath her stepmother's intuitive stare, she swallowed and tried again. "You're not a burden on me."

"What a sweet child you are," said Marielle.

A shiver pulsed up Eugenie's spine. Why had she never discerned that note of contempt in her stepmother's voice?

11

Smoke and Shadow

Florelle and Aurielle bickered like a pair of posturing hens for the next hour. Eugenie, counting down the time to her appointed meeting with Pip, lingered near the stairs to keep tabs on their whereabouts and her stepmother's. Marielle had not come upstairs. She had not, as far as Eugenie knew, left the kitchen after putting away the groceries.

Was that strange behavior? After two solid weeks spent in her workroom, she couldn't recall her stepmother's daily habits. Her nerves drew tight as the shadows stretched longer and longer across the entryway below. The squabble across the hall was almost a relief.

"I already *said* I was wearing lavender. You can't wear *any* shade of purple."

"You don't own the whole color."

"Oh, wear your old gold dress. It suits you better than that puce monstrosity anyway."

"You just want me to look scuffed so you can shine."

Did they really believe they could fool anyone? It was one thing to go to court to see whether a mystery girl showed up, but to claim her identity as their own ... How would Prince Fernand react if Florelle managed to stuff her foot into the rigid quartz shoe? And if she failed? Would the queen see it as attempted fraud against the crown?

But the Elles might not be the only ones who entertained such a scheme. If the true owner never appeared, nothing would stop someone from claiming her spot. The shoe might fit any number of ladies across the kingdom.

What responsibility did Eugenie bear in this terrible mix-up? Surely Pip would guide her in what to do.

If he kept their meeting.

When the last light of day slipped away into twilight, she stole from her hiding place and down the stairs, her heart in her throat. A self-conscious glance at the hall leading toward the kitchen showed it deserted. She tossed her cloak around her shoulders and donned her shoes.

Even as she grasped the knob, it turned in her hand. She wrenched back as the front door swung inward. "Oh!"

Marielle paused on the threshold, her eyes huge. She wore her dark cloak, her hair wind-ruffled beneath the hood. "Are you going somewhere?" she asked, eyeing her stepdaughter up and down.

Eugenie clutched the ties at her throat. "To ... to the chickens. To see if any laid this afternoon." Her stepmother lifted her chin as though enlightened, which prompted her to add, "I didn't know you had gone out."

"Yes, down to the inn to reserve a carriage for tomorrow."

"Oh, of course," said Eugenie.

"I suppose you disapprove," Marielle said, her mouth curving in a faint smile.

"I—"

She tilted her head as though contrite. "Don't judge us too harshly. You don't know what it's like to have an uncertain future. Sometimes you have to take your chances to survive."

In former days, Eugenie would have reassured her stepmother. Despite Pip's charge for her to act natural, she could not force such words to cross her lips. Instead, she said, "I'm just worried. What happens to Florelle and Aurielle if their foot doesn't fit? Will the queen be angry?"

"Psh," said Marielle with a dismissive wave. "Court will be packed tomorrow with claimants. It will become a sport among the nobles, with lords placing wagers while ladies stand in line."

Eugenie nodded and moved again toward the door, eager to end the conversation.

"Why do you not use the door off the kitchen?" Marielle asked.

Eugenie's hand trembled on the knob. She forced a carefree smile. "I like to walk through the garden."

Her stepmother's expression remained steady, observing. "Well," the woman said at last, "steer clear of the pond or any other puddles that may yet lurk from the rain. I don't know how many more baptisms your shoes can withstand before we get you another pair."

A feeble chuckle worked from her throat. She ducked her head in acknowledgement and scuttled out the door.

Heavy clouds yet hung in the purple sky. She bundled her cloak closer and hurried around the side of the house, certain she could feel the weight of Marielle's gaze upon her with every step. She dared not chance a look toward the windows to confirm, but she caught movement of the curtains in her periphery.

If Pip awaited her in the garden, as he'd said, they would have no privacy. She continued quickly to the back of the house, to the coop that lay beyond the barn. The birds, gathered within for the night, chirred protests as she reached beneath them in their boxes. She slipped the full clutch of eggs—most of which she should have collected that morning while her stepmother and stepsisters slept—into her apron pockets.

Marielle would know from the sheer volume that she had not completed that task, which might lead to unwanted questions. Paranoid, Eugenie contemplated chucking some of them into the pond before she returned to the house.

As she stepped out of the coop, a voice whispered from the shadows around her.

"You're a blessed sight, Eugenie."

Pip emerged in a rustle from among the nearby shrubbery. She gasped and dragged him behind the coop, her watchful eyes searching the path back to the manor.

"What's wrong?" he asked, close enough that she could feel his warmth. "There's no one else out here. I watched to make sure no one followed you."

Her shoulders sagged on a sigh of relief. "I think Marielle might suspect something," she said, stricken. "She's paying special attention to everything I do. She told the younger Elles that they would all skip the next masquerade and insisted I rest, which *seems* innocent enough, but—"

"Do you want to come away with me tonight?" he asked. His eyes gleamed in the low light.

Eugenie studied him. "Is that your plan? To spirit me off in darkness?"

"No, but if you're worried, I'll drop everything and take you away."

His mere presence restored her lost equilibrium. The panic that had fluttered through her veins all afternoon subsided, and her breath evened to a calm rhythm.

"What was your plan?" she asked.

"Oh, it's brilliant. I went straight from you to the queen."

Her anxiety sparked. "That's something else! The queen sent out a proclamation this afternoon, that the lady of the shoe is to present herself in court tomorrow to... to..." She couldn't complete the sentence about claiming Prince Fernand's heart, but she didn't need to. A broad grin split Pip's face and he quivered with ill-suppressed mirth. Mystified, she asked, "Why are you laughing?"

"That's my doing, the proclamation," he said. "I told Her Royal Majesty everything. The whole proclamation is a ruse. I'm only relieved that word of it reached the manor house so quickly."

"It's not funny, Pip. Marielle has convinced Florelle and Aurielle to try on the shoe for themselves."

"As I intended. No, listen: they'll be gone the whole day, which gives us plenty of time to collect your personal effects and steal you away from that wicked woman's clutches."

He had created a window of opportunity where they would have no fear of Marielle's eminent return. Even as she marveled at the simplicity of it, anxiety for its possible side-effects shot through her. "But what if one of them fits the shoe? Will Prince Fernand have to honor his word?"

"Prince Fernand is a willing party to the whole of it," he said, though with a flash of exasperation. "Besides, any claimant that fits the shoe will have to rescind her claim when you show up with the match."

Eugenie squeaked. "What? I can't—"

Pip grasped her wrists, his gaze intent. "The queen is willing to believe you are who you say on my word alone. But as your funeral was a public event, she demands that your return to society be public as well, that all the ranks of the nation acknowledge the House of Pluterra restored before their very eyes."

Her throat constricted at the grandiose image he painted, and of how ill she fit it. "I have nothing to wear to court. All my clothes are threadbare. I'll look like a peasant among that crowd."

"So look like a peasant. Come in sackcloth and ashes. It'll confirm the baroness's crimes all the more." When his words failed to reassure her, he pressed her hands. "Your clothes don't determine your rank in the world, Eugenie."

"I know. I wouldn't mind if I could go in private, but to present myself before all the nobles of the court—"

"Baroness Lavande *must* have a public reckoning. That was the queen's own condition. If you come to court away from the eyes of the nation, there's nothing to stop your stepmother from fleeing the country. This way, she presents herself into our midst, never suspecting the trap that awaits."

The plan was a cunning stroke. It left Eugenie breathless, struggling against instinctive guilt for springing a snare against one who had often treated her with kindness. Had she not seen her name carved into her parents' memorial she might still believe her stepmother's treachery a fantastic lie.

But what if Marielle caught wind beforehand? Her keen eyes always observed and assessed. What if she could read into her stepdaughter's very soul?

"I'm a little afraid," Eugenie admitted.

He squeezed her hands again. "Every masquerade has to have an unmasking at its end. The baroness has played this game far too long to get away with it. Tomorrow, if all goes well, she'll finish the day inside a prison cell."

Would that be the end of everything? Even if the queen

believed Eugenie, would the rest of Jacondria? What of the people of her own village, who thought she was the housemaid Nanette?

"Have you heard anything from Theo?" she asked, her voice barely above a whisper.

"Not yet. He'll turn up eventually. And when he does, I'll make sure he begs your forgiveness."

She chuckled, but half-heartedly. On her backward step, the manor house slid into view. Lantern light burned in the younger Elles' windows on the upper level, but Marielle's was yet dark.

"I should go back before she comes looking for me."

His lips parted to respond, but her next realization cut him short.

"Oh! Here." She pulled eggs from her apron pockets and set them in his hands, three in each.

He stared down, bewildered. "What am I supposed to do with these?"

She frowned. "You eat them. Haven't you eaten eggs before?"

He huffed a laugh. "Yes, but—"

"I should've collected most of them while the Elles were sleeping today. If I come back with the whole batch, Marielle will know I didn't, and she'll ask about what I did this morning. So you get to take those." She backed away toward the house, not ready to turn from him yet.

A smile tugged at the corners of his mouth, though bemusement still possessed him. "Eugenie," he said as one newly enlightened, "I know this is not the right time, but you are absolutely adorable."

Her heart and her face burned. She thanked the shadows for hiding her heightened color. "Why would this not be the right time?"

"Because you're in the midst of a crisis. And yet"—he raised both hands full of eggs—"you charm me nonetheless."

Crisis or not, she loved him. The knowledge struck her like a bolt of lightning from the lowering clouds above and robbed her of any coherent response.

He called *her* charming? He radiated the stuff. It infused him from top to toe, ensnaring anyone lucky enough to encounter him.

"I'm coming for you tomorrow," he said. "Expect me as soon as the baroness and her daughters are gone. Until then, be safe."

She nodded, her heart too full to speak more than a hurried goodnight. She bolted up the path to the house, single-minded in reaching that goal, of shutting herself up in her room to sift through these new feelings.

Of course she loved Pip. She had loved him from the first masquerade, but that had been a shallow, frivolous love. This— *this* possessed her senses beyond anything she could describe. It burned within, filling her with determination to merit whatever he felt for her, whether trivial or great.

She swung the front door inward to a dark entryway. Light spilled from the younger Elles' rooms into the hallway above. Eugenie started toward the kitchen.

"What took so long?"

She shrieked and spun, her pulse galloping in her throat. Marielle stood within the door to the front room, shielding the dull light from a lantern trimmed low. Its meager flame cast her pretty face into ghastly, hellish relief. At her stepdaughter's outburst, her brows arched. "Did I frighten you?"

Eugenie, panting, scrambled for an excuse. "I'm sorry. I think I spooked myself out there. I should have gone before the sun was down."

"You were gone so long that I wondered if I ought to send one of the girls after you."

"I was . . . lost in my thoughts, I guess."

Marielle drew closer. "And what thoughts occupied you so fully?"

Conscious of a pressing desire to escape, Eugenie willed her feet not to move. "Costume ideas. Dragonflies, and water sprites, and cypress trees, and how I might create any of them in a gown."

"I told you not to worry about that this week," her stepmother said, her voice light. "If the prince finds his bride tomorrow, it's unlikely the palace will hold another masquerade anytime soon. They'll focus on a royal wedding instead."

"Of course," said Eugenie. "How stupid of me."

"Do you want to try on the slipper?"

The question caught her off-guard. She started, then took a defensive step backward. "No. I wasn't at the masquerade."

"No one knows that," said Marielle. The corners of her lips tipped upward in an encouraging smile.

What did she suspect? Had she found the hidden shoe? Surely not—

"I don't want to interfere," Eugenie said.

"And I suppose there's no reason you should. How many eggs were there?"

Wordlessly she lifted the remaining four from her pockets, grateful she had passed the majority to Pip before coming inside.

Marielle pursed her lips in what was almost a lop-sided pout. "Into the basket with them, and then up to bed. We have to wake up early, and you know how the girls depend on you to look their best. You don't mind, do you?"

"No," said Eugenie. For once she would be eager to get the whole lot of them out of the house.

12
Amid the Ashes

FLORELLE'S LAVENDER GOWN had a tear in the sleeve, and Aurielle's chosen dress, in aqua blue, had a dribble of egg yolk on the flouncing skirt. Despite Marielle's charge to go to bed early, Eugenie stayed up in her workroom to complete these tasks. Her lantern burned bright and she kept one eye on the door and the darkened hallway beyond. When she had pressed both frocks and starched the underskirts, she hung them up and banked the coals in her small workroom fireplace. She did the same in the front room and the kitchen, checking over her shoulder as she collected excess ashes into their respective bins.

Every shadow crawled with untold malice. She crept upstairs to her own room and stoked the fire in her grate. As she drifted off to sleep in the dim glow, she pulled her covers to her chin as if to guard against any harm. Dawn, only a few hours later, poured feeble light and birdsong into her room. She awoke to Marielle beside her bed, a neutral expression on the woman's face.

Eugenie, stiff as a board and every fine hair standing on end, stared up at her.

"You didn't wake when I knocked," her stepmother said in her feathery voice. She was already dressed in a dark green gown, its color a compliment to her beauty, though her pale hair yet hung in waves over one shoulder. "The girls need your help tightening their stays."

"Of course." Eugenie scrambled from beneath her covers and out her bedroom door, conscious of the stare that bored into her spine. She found the younger Elles squabbling as usual, each refusing to help the other lace up her underthings. Quietly she went to work.

Sometime in the many layers that followed, she stole away to change from her thin nightgown into the least threadbare of her work dresses. A patchwork of faded blues and whites, it was a far cry from the gorgeous ensembles her stepsisters and everyone else would wear to court.

"You've tied Aurielle tighter than me," Florelle complained when she returned.

"If she ties you any tighter, you'll break a rib," her sister said. Eugenie ushered Aurielle to the vanity, hopeful of distracting any further argument, but Aurielle slung one more barb over her shoulder. "It's not her fault you're built like a tree trunk, with not a curve in sight."

Florelle was ready for her. "At least my posture's not hunched. If your shoulders were any more sloped, the mice could sled off them come wintertime."

"Will you have time to eat breakfast before your carriage comes?" Eugenie asked as Aurielle's outrage manifested in a shriek. "Should I fix you something?"

Aurielle transferred her ire, sneering at her stepsister's reflection in the mirror. "What, so I can spill egg on my dress again?"

"You think I can swallow a bite when I'm trussed up like

this?" Florelle asked behind her. "You've obviously never worn anything tighter than that sack you're wearing now."

Her fairy-costumes had been not at all constricting—doubtless thanks to the magic that constructed them—so Eugenie said with complete honesty, "No, I haven't." She brushed Aurielle's thin hair into a tail and twisted it upward.

Florelle harrumphed. "You wouldn't suggest something as stupid as breakfast if you had. If you're so hungry, you can eat as soon as we leave."

Eugenie perched three hairpins between her lips so she wouldn't have to respond.

Marielle, who had been conspicuously absent from her daughters' preparations, appeared now with a basket of flowers from the garden, freshly cut to fit into the younger Elles' coiffures. "I've gathered the morning eggs as well," she said to her stepdaughter, whose brows arched. None of the Elles ever collected the eggs. Marielle continued. "I think there must be tramps cutting through our garden at night. There were boot prints in the mud that were too big to belong to any of us."

"Are you sure?" Aurielle slid a snide glance toward her sister's feet.

"I'm sure," her mother said before Florelle could bristle. The tone of her voice warned against any further quips, deadly serious. "Eugenie, you didn't see anyone out there last night, did you?"

Startled, Eugenie jabbed a pin into Aurielle's scalp. Her stepsister yowled. "Watch what you're doing!"

"No," she said, meeting Marielle's gaze in the mirror and averting her own again. "Do you think someone was out there the same time I was?"

"It's possible. You should be careful, especially going out after dark." The words sounded light, but Marielle's expression remained piercing. A chill swept over Eugenie. Her hands shook as she coiled a strand of hair into a curl.

The tension broke when Florelle loudly asked, "How long are you going to take over there? I need my hair done too, you know."

Marielle ushered her to the opposite vanity and started the task herself. Silence enveloped the room, broken only when one of the younger Elles demanded a certain flower for her hair. Half the garden sprung from their upward twists before they were satisfied.

"There's one left for you," Marielle said to Eugenie, pulling a battered carnation from the bottom of the basket.

Had she always carried such veiled hostility? Eugenie took the broken stem with a forced smile and snapped the lower half off. The flower, half-crushed, she tucked into her apron belt.

Florelle and Aurielle were already pulling their wraps around their shoulders, giddy with anticipation for what the day would hold. Through the open window floated the sound of a carriage rattling up the drive.

"Are you sure you don't want to come try this slipper on for yourself?" Marielle asked.

Her daughters gaped.

"She *can't*," Florelle said.

Aurielle thrust an elbow into her ribcage and added, "Not wearing *that*. And the hackney's already here. There's no time for her to change."

"It can stand at the door," said Marielle, her gaze never leaving her stepdaughter's face.

Eugenie swallowed. "I don't want to go. But good luck."

"You'll see us out, as always?"

Unable to decline, she followed her stepmother and stepsisters downstairs to the front door.

"Remember you're supposed to be resting," Marielle said as she pulled dark gloves onto her hands. "Don't do anything foolish while we're gone." She passed outside behind her girls. Eugenie, cold with anxiety, hung upon the door frame as they climbed into their coach. She almost shut the door when the horses turned back up the lane but belatedly recalled that she always watched.

As the carriage passed the fence posts, Marielle looked back. For the first time ever.

Even from that distance, hatred shot from her like an arrow straight into Eugenie's heart. It was only for an instant before she disappeared onto the road. A trick of imagination, perhaps? But Eugenie could not dismiss the warning that flashed through her.

Heart in her throat, she fled to the front room, to the ash bin by the hearth. She dumped it over, spilling the contents across the flagstones.

Amid the mess, beneath a coat of fine debris, the second slipper gleamed.

She breathed a sigh of relief. If Marielle had been snooping, at least she hadn't found this incriminating piece.

A clatter of wheels outside pulled her toward the window. Had they returned, or—?

But the carriage that pulled up to the door now was not the same hackney they had left in. It was the one from the cemetery, complete with the pair of black horses.

Before the footman could alight from the back, the door opened and Pip hopped to the ground.

He had told her to expect him as soon as the Elles left, hadn't he? Sweet relief flooded through Eugenie as she darted to the entryway to let him in.

Pip grinned as he crossed the threshold. "You'll never know how glad I am to see you whole and healthy," he said. "I've passed the most wretched night convinced I should have stolen you away yesterday." He motioned through the open door for his driver to wait, and then shut it tight.

Eugenie tucked a stray strand of hair behind one ear, self-conscious. "Marielle suspects something. I'm half-terrified that she'll turn around and come back for me. She asked me twice whether I wanted to go to court to try on the slipper for myself. She collected the eggs this morning, which she never does, and found your boot prints in the mud."

He sobered, but brushed off any additional concern. "She wouldn't know they were *my* boot prints."

"No. She told us to watch out for tramps crossing the estate."

That elicited a laugh. He clasped her hand, his warmth transferring through his white gloves. His clothes, in their understated fineness, created a stark contrast to hers.

"Let's collect your things and be gone, the sooner the better," he said.

She left a smear of ash upon his glove when she withdrew her hand. What was she doing, keeping company with someone so far above her?

"This way," she said and led him further into the house.

They collected her sketchbooks from her workroom, stashing them in an old satchel of her father's. Next, in her bedroom, she pulled a pair of diaries she had kept. Pip watched in bemusement as she dropped to the floor to fish beneath her bed. When she withdrew a packet of letters, he frowned.

"They're from the prince," she said.

He snatched the bundle from her hands, studying the address on the topmost one. "You kept them?"

She tipped her head, confused at the catch in his voice. "Why wouldn't I?"

He thumbed the edges of the stack as though counting them. "You spoke yesterday like they were nothing important."

Did he worry that she harbored a tenderness for the prince? To be sure, she had adored the stalwart boy of a decade ago, but as an acolyte might adore an icon. Those letters, formal though they had been from one whose rank so eclipsed her own, had provided spots of brightness in an otherwise dim period of her life. "They were important," she said quietly, apologetically. "He wrote again when my father died, but it was to the whole family. Florelle has that one somewhere. I kept these apart."

"You said at the masquerade that you didn't want to meet him again," said Pip, worry in his eyes.

A blush crawled up her neck. She averted her gaze to the window. "He won't be the same now as he was then. He can't be. Sometimes, when you want to keep something precious, you guard it against change." She chanced a peek at him; he looked thunderstruck—dismayed?—his lips parted but with no voice. Guilt pulsed through her. "Is it bad that I kept his letters?"

Pip shook off his stupor. "No, it's good. Of course it's good. The queen has already accepted my word, but if you have these, then that's all the more proof."

"Maybe they'll jar the prince's memory," said Eugenie.

"His memory doesn't need jarring," said Pip, tossing the letters into the bag with everything else. "You can claim your birthright on your own merit, but a handful of old letters won't hurt your cause. Is there anything else?"

"My family's portrait in the gallery," she said. "I was only a child when it was painted, though."

He motioned her toward the hall. "Lead the way."

The portrait gallery, easily the largest room in the manor, stretched along the back on the second floor, its high walls featuring kindred of the House of Pluterra from hundreds of years back. Bygone fashions and noble hobbies graced the subjects, pictured riding or dancing or ensconced amid emblems of their earthly life. Eugenie stopped near the center, in front of an image that the other portraits fairly dwarfed.

Small though it was, the frame was solid and ornate. She hefted it from the wall. "My father was going to have a larger one painted, but my mother fell ill. It became more important to finish it before she passed, so that she could see us all together." Her fingertips grazed her mother's lovely face. Her father stood with dignity beside the seated woman. The child-Eugenie between them was round-cheeked, with the rosy blush of youth upon her.

She crushed her welling emotions, determined not to cry.

Tucking the painting under one arm, she led the way back downstairs. She stacked it next to the door and glanced around the entryway, as though to memorize every hairline crack in the mortared walls.

"Where's the other slipper?" Pip asked.

"In the front room. I was getting it when you arrived."

He crossed to the threshold but paused, observing the mess of cinders upon the hearth.

Eugenie joined him. "I buried it in the ash bin. Marielle won't touch ashes—she abhors them."

Had the fairy known that detail? Perhaps she had dressed Eugenie as soot because Marielle hated her too. On this sober thought, she crossed to the fireplace and picked up the cinder-covered slipper. "It's a bit dingy," she said, rubbing it against her apron.

Soot and Slipper

"It's exquisite, regardless of its environ," Pip replied. He plucked it from her hands, turning it over as he inspected it.

Her throat tightened. "You're getting soot all over your gloves."

In answer, he wiped the slipper clean, dirtying the pristine white fabric and favoring her with a defiant glance in the process. She suppressed a laugh. When he returned the shoe to her, she slipped it into her apron pocket. He, meanwhile, removed his gloves and tucked them into his belt.

Upon a trembling sigh, she surveyed the front room one last time. An ironic chuckle escaped her lips. "I think that's everything I need. If you see anything here you want, feel free to take it."

Pip swept her off her feet. She squeaked and looped her arms around his neck to steady herself, gaping up at him with huge, wondering eyes.

He carried her to the entryway. "You don't technically qualify as a thing," he said with a wry smile, "but I didn't want to take any chances."

Her heart might have burst, both broken and patched at the same time. The emotion she had fought spilled over. She tightened her hold and buried her face against his shoulder on a sob. The hands that carried her tucked her close, enveloping her in safety.

When he paused at the front door, she wiped her tears with one hurried wrist. "I'm sorry. It's just . . . it's been so long since anyone wanted me." Embarrassed by the admission and her lack of emotional control, she angled away to rub her face against the collar of her dress.

Gently he set her on her own two feet. His hands remained looped around her waist. "That's not entirely true," he said, as though choosing his words with utmost care. "I wanted you from the moment we first met, as a friend if nothing more."

Disbelief shot through her. She jerked her attention to him but found only sincerity in his eyes.

What had she done to deserve such faithfulness? And how could she possibly express her own? He was so close. It felt completely natural to perch on her tiptoes and brush a kiss against his lips.

His mouth followed her retreat. The arms around her waist drew her in; her own tightened their loop around his neck. The kiss deepened, unhampered by silly half-masks or fears of judgement.

"Eugenie, you must know I love you," he said on a desperate, panting breath.

A feather-light laugh escaped her. "Then why are you making me try on shoes for the prince?"

He kissed her again, more insistent this time. She wrapped him all the closer, alive in his embrace.

13
Into the Fire

"Everything is going to change from this moment forward," said Pip as the black carriage glided into the palace estate.

Eugenie, cradled against him, stiffened. "Does it have to be a public affair? I don't mind if Marielle gets away."

"I mind," said Pip. "If you won't demand justice for her crimes against you, I will."

A hundred or more carriages lined the drive, their horses and liverymen idle as they awaited their masters' leisure. All of Jacondria had assembled before the queen, it seemed. Pip's coach rolled into the courtyard, and Eugenie tensed. His protective arm around her provided her only solace.

The carriage stopped in front of the grand staircase. Pip leapt down and helped her descend. A faint tremor in his hand spiked her anxiety all the more. He hid his nerves well, but not completely.

When a pair of palace guards approached, he gestured to the items left in the coach. "The queen has asked that the bag and the picture be taken to her private chambers for safekeeping."

The guards immediately complied.

"Did she really?" Eugenie whispered in awe.

"I'm sure she would've if she'd thought of it," said Pip with a wry smile.

Her stomach twisted in knots. They were taking a lot of liberties and trusting the crown not to retaliate.

She climbed the guard-lined stairs on his arm, conscious of the many critical glances upon her. Her tattered cloak swished around her calves, her dress short enough to expose her ankles and her thin, worn shoes. Her golden hair, though neat and clean, hung in its loose, natural curls down to her shoulder blades. She had not thought to pull it up until this very moment.

As they crossed the threshold into the cool palace interior, a royal steward stepped forward.

"Don't announce us," said Pip, raising one hand to ward the man off. "I'll do it myself." To Eugenie's curious look he added, "Remember, just as we planned. Straight to the pedestal and put the other slipper there."

A roar of conversation traveled up from the great hall. She had expected a line of hopefuls already trying on the infamous shoe, but it stood untouched upon a marble column in front of the royal dais. Queen Patrice and her consort, Prince Renaud, sat regal in their thrones, but Prince Fernand's place was empty.

Perhaps they waited for his arrival to begin.

"Deep breath," said Pip, steeling his own nerves as much as Eugenie's.

They descended the stairs, each trembling and simultaneously drawing support from the other. A hush rippled through the assembled nobles. They parted, creating a pathway for the strange pair. Eugenie heard a gasp from somewhere to her left and recognized it as one of the younger Elles, but she dared not stray her gaze from the throne directly ahead.

The Queen of Jacondria, proud and austere, stared straight at her. She was exactly as Eugenie remembered, an intimidating presence in her royal finery, starched to a perfect point with not a hair out of place beneath her heavy, jeweled crown.

They reached the pedestal. Eugenie dropped her gaze at last. Her pulse jittering in her veins, she extracted the missing slipper from her apron and set it carefully beside its mate.

A knife could have cut through the silence of the room, so palpable it was.

Pip cleared his throat, the sound almost jarring. "It is my honor to present to queen and country Eugenie Vivienne, the Marchioness of Pluterra."

Sharp inhales punctured the room. The crowd erupted in murmurs, their gazes flitting from Eugenie to a point left and behind her—to Baroness Lavande in their midst.

The queen raised her hand, motioning for silence. Sympathy flashed through her eyes as she looked upon Eugenie, but then she shifted her attention to Pip. When she spoke, it was in a voice of quiet reproof.

"Fernand, take your rightful place."

Eugenie jolted. In horror she gaped up at Pip, who met her stare with an apologetic expression. He squeezed her hand in reassurance and then left her—*abandoned* her—to mount the royal dais.

A glance around the room showed no one else surprised. They all knew who he was. She alone had been ignorant—ridiculously so.

Mortified, she clenched her hands together. Prince Fernand tried to catch her gaze from where he sat upon his throne, but she lowered her attention to the floor, embarrassment burning her ears.

"Baroness Lavande," said the queen, "I believe you owe us an explanation."

Rustling behind Eugenie signaled a parting of the crowd. Marielle's footsteps tapped across the marble floor. Eugenie's skin crawled as her stepmother came to stand beside her.

"Please, Your Majesty," said Marielle in her sweetest, most importuning voice, "you mustn't blame her. The poor girl was taken ill and hasn't been right in the head since."

Eugenie snapped her attention from her feet to her stepmother's profile, but Marielle never looked away from the queen as she continued.

"It was my fault—entirely my fault. I allowed her to nurse our sweet Eugenie in her final days, and when she caught the sickness herself, she never quite recovered from the delirium it brought. We've kept her on the estate, hoping in some part to repay the sacrifice she made for us and to shelter her from embarrassment."

Horror washed over Eugenie—doubly so when the queen asked, "Then you claim this is not Eugenie of Pluterra?"

Marielle shook her head, the picture of contrition. "She gets upset if we don't call her Eugenie, but in truth, she is only our maid, Nanette."

Eugenie recoiled. "I am not!"

"You see, Your Majesty?" said Marielle, triumph tugging at the corners of her mouth.

"I'm not Nanette!" Eugenie cried. "Nanette left us years ago. I'm Eugenie!"

Her stepmother placed a soothing hand upon her arm. "Shh, I know. We'll get this settled and get you home, poor child."

Eugenie ripped away from her touch, conscious of a hundred or more critical stares upon her. Marielle's thorn of doubt had struck its mark. The queen remained unmoved, except for one hand upon her son's wrist. Pip, agitated, looked as though he would fly from his chair if not for that simple restraint.

"My daughters can verify the truth," said Marielle, gesturing behind her. Florelle and Aurielle, at the edge of the nobles, nodded vigorously.

"That's right," said Florelle. "She's only Nanette."

"She's never been right in the head, not since she was taken so ill, poor thing," said Aurielle.

Murmurs erupted anew and the uncertainty of the crowd redoubled.

The queen spoke above the din. "Their testimony is noted, but it cannot be taken as absolute proof. Filial loyalty renders it suspect."

"Forgive me," said Marielle, bowing her head. She sniffled, and a crystalline teardrop escaped to drop upon the floor. She dabbed at her eyes with a delicate handkerchief. "This is all very upsetting. It was difficult enough to lose our Eugenie, but now poor Nanette, who doesn't even know what she's doing, would convince you—what? That I faked my stepdaughter's death? Am I such a monster?"

"I'm not dead, and I'm not Nanette!" Eugenie cried, more and more flustered.

"It's all right, dear," said Marielle, soothing through her tears. "Florie and Aurie will get you home if I cannot. You'll be back in your sewing room in no time, drawing your pretty patterns."

"She knows things that no mere maid would know," said Pip, his voice tight and his fists clenched.

"Eugenie told her *everything*," said Marielle. "I thought nothing of it at the time. Only in her recovery, when the injury to her brain became apparent—"

"I don't have an injury to my brain!"

"No, of course. You're perfectly fine, sweet girl. Your Majesty, please, she'll only become more agitated the longer this goes on. She's as innocent as an infant and has no clue what sort of tricks she's played."

Fear cinched Eugenie's lungs tight. The nobles around her looked upon her with mingled contempt and pity. Marielle, in all her soft-spoken refinement, looked like the picture of honesty and compassion. Light-headedness struck, and she fought against its dizzying effects.

Almost she doubted herself. *Could it be possible—?*

"She's not Nanette," said Pip from his throne, his teeth clenched.

Marielle humbly inclined her head. "Forgive her, please, Your Highness."

He started up, but his mother clamped her hand upon his arm and sent him a warning glance. A mute power struggle passed between them.

At long last, she returned her attention to the petite blonde before her. "These charges are grave, Baroness."

"Indeed."

"What proof have you that she is a maid and not your stepdaughter?"

Triumph flashed in Marielle's eyes as she lifted her gaze from the floor. "I send her wages to her parents every month. If you will but dispatch a messenger to them, they will verify that their daughter, Nanette, works for me. The whole of Hazelcross village knows it too. As for her being my stepdaughter..." A short, disbelieving laugh crossed her lips. She surveyed the crowd, soliciting their support. "Almost everyone in this room attended Eugenie's funeral. The royal coroner signed her death notice. Her name is inscribed with her parents' names upon their memorial."

Eugenie trembled beneath the weight of her stepmother's words, that her deception could be so complete. "It's not true," she whispered. She looked to her stepsisters. "Florelle, Aurielle, please—"

Both girls refused to meet her gaze, their spines stiff as they stared straight ahead.

"Marielle, please don't do this," Eugenie said.

Her stepmother spared her a piteous sidelong glance and only said, "Send a messenger to Nanette's parents, Your Majesty. You will have the truth from them."

But before Queen Patrice could respond, a cheerful voice rang out at the top of the stairs. "No need to send someone. I've gone and brought them here."

14
Combustion

"Lord Theophilus Pierrick Sebastien Alexis Michel, Fifth Earl of Mereloye," said the royal herald in sonorous tones, "with Joseph and Sarah of Netherford Village."

Theo disappeared and then returned to usher a humble couple—somewhere between fifty and sixty years old—down the stairs. In dress they were no more elaborate than Eugenie, their clothing worn and their faces lined with years of labor. She studied the pair, seeking even a glimpse of recognition in them. Some strange familiarity tugged at her, something in the spread of the husband's nose and the curve of his wife's neck.

Her discomfort simmered. Why should she recognize people she had never seen before? Was her memory of Nanette playing tricks on her, the daughter's inherited features manifested upon her parents' faces?

They gaped at the company of nobles, clinging to one another as they reached the last step.

"I did what you told me to, Nic," said Theo just behind them. "Don't be angry at the outcome."

"I won't," said Pip, his attention on Marielle.

Soot and Slipper

Eugenie looked to her stepmother, who forced a pleasant smile even though the blood had drained completely from her face. As the couple approached the throne, she edged toward the crowd.

They dropped into an awkward bow and curtsy before the queen.

"You are the parents of the maid, Nanette, who works for Baroness Lavande?" she asked.

"Yes, ma'am—Your Majesty, yes," said the husband. "Our Nanette has worked for the baroness these past four years."

"And you receive her wages for her?"

"Every month she sends what she can," he said.

"She's a good girl, our Nanette," said his wife, her voice faltering.

"And when was the last time you saw her?"

"She don't come away from the manor house," said the husband.

"Do you see her here?" asked the queen.

The pair looked around the room with wide, searching eyes. Their gaze slid right past Eugenie as they peered among the nobles.

"Is our Nanette here?" asked the wife.

The crowd murmured, glancing from Eugenie to Marielle, who now could not melt into their ranks.

The baroness straightened, answering the challenge. "Her appearance has changed in the past four years, Your Majesty, as is common in girls her age."

The queen gestured the couple to look at Eugenie. "Is this your Nanette?"

They recoiled. "No," said the man.

"Not our Nanette," said his wife.

"Your Majesty—" the baroness began, but Queen Patrice cut her off with a raised hand.

"Are you sure?" she asked the pair.

"Begging your pardon." The husband wrung his hat in his hands. "She's nothing like our Nanette."

"We couldn't give our children such pretty looks," said the wife. "We gave them pretty names instead. Our Nanette is a good girl, but she's plain, and humble about it. Where is she, please?"

The question hung upon the air. Dread took root in Eugenie's soul, as the only logical conclusion surfaced. The queen spared a sidelong glance to her prince consort, who squeezed her hand in reassurance. "Baroness?"

Marielle only shook her head, her face ashen.

"I regret to inform you," said the queen to the couple, "that in all likelihood, your Nanette has died and was buried three years ago in another person's grave."

The whole court erupted. A wail of anguish burst from the mother's lips. "No! Not our Nanette! Two daughters taken from us? It is too much to bear! Too much!"

The queen, in concern, sat forward on her throne. "Two daughters?"

"Begging your pardon, Majesty," said the heartbroken husband as he cradled his sobbing wife. "Our oldest child disappeared when our Nanette was just a babe. We've never learned what happened to her yet, though it's certain she fell afoul of some wandering rogues. Hush, Sarah," he cooed to his wife. "We'll add Nanette's memorial to Marielle's."

Shock thrummed through Eugenie, one of the few people close enough to hear this reassurance. "Marielle?" she said sharply. Her attention snapped to her stepmother, who stood frozen across from her. She looked at Eugenie with bloodless hatred in the thinning of her lips. Almost imperceptibly she shook her head.

Could it be—?

"Is that your Marielle?" Eugenie asked the grieving pair.

"Of course I'm not," her stepmother snapped. "There's more than one Marielle in the country, you stupid girl."

The couple looked up, but no sign of recognition manifested on their faces. "That's not our Marielle," said the husband.

Triumph flashed across the baroness's face.

"She's much too pretty," said the wife, and the triumph vanished into livid rage.

"No!" Marielle shrieked, and she stamped her foot. "Don't say it like that!"

A peal of laughter echoed through the hall, reverberating through all who heard it. Otherworldly, it cut through the tumult of confusion. A hundred nobles looked to the ceiling, to a whirling ball of magic with a firefly heart. It plunged and landed beside the pedestal where the quartz shoes yet rested. Sparks burst from the impact, and a humanoid figure blossomed in their midst, with fiery red hair and merriment plain upon her face.

Eugenie's throat constricted.

"You walked right into that one, little soot-ling," said the fairy godmother with a giant grin. She spoke not to Eugenie, but to Marielle.

The baroness replied through clenched teeth. "You *cheated*."

The dainty creature pranced forward in a silent jig. "Fairies can't cheat. We make the rules."

Upon her throne, the queen chose her words with utmost care. "To what do we owe this most noble visit?"

"I'm here to collect my own," said the fairy with a dimpled smile. "Beauty for ashes—that was our bargain, was it not?" This question, directed toward Marielle, received no response. Unperturbed, the fairy returned her attention to the queen. "She's fairy-cursed, this one, and of her own making. She wanted a pretty face, but everything comes with a price. Was it worth it, soot-ling?"

Marielle quivered, her hands clenched.

"What was the price?" asked the queen.

"Beauty for ashes, as I said. Everything she gets with that pretty face turns to naught." The fairy shifted a mocking look upon the baroness. "She snagged herself a baron, and it led to ugly babies and a ruined fortune." She broke off in a merry laugh.

Florelle and Aurielle, further down the line from their mother, squeaked their faint protest.

The fairy continued her taunting. "And her second husband doted so much on his first wife and child that he refused to muddy the inheritance with another heir. Too bad, soot-ling. You should have taken your price with good humor. But then you played a nasty trick: you stole a fortune not by your looks, but by your wits."

The crowd, captivated by this unfolding of events, shifted their attention to Marielle for her response.

She trembled with rage. "You cheated. You interfered." She flung a finger toward Eugenie. "You sent that little brat to the masquerade? That violates our bargain!"

"Hmm, no." The fairy bestowed a sickly sweet smile upon her. "She always thought you were beautiful. I had every right to incinerate that—just like I can't let you escape recognition now by your looks. Ashes, ashes, it all turns to ashes," she finished in a sing-song voice.

Horror plunged across Marielle. "No," she cried.

Soot and Slipper

"Yes," said the fairy with a grin as broad as a jousting field. "I'm afraid our bargain has reached its end. It's been a delight, little soot-ling—for me, at least." She flicked her wrist, and magic flared around the baroness.

Marielle shrieked and covered her face. Those near her retreated as the fairy-spell twisted upward. It left behind a quivering woman with streaks of gray shot through her mouse-brown hair. She peered through trembling fingers, her eyes slate-colored.

"Marielle," said Joseph of Netherford in wonder.

"Don't look at me!" she screamed, and she backed away when he took a stilted step toward her. The whole room hushed, waiting for her next move. She slowly withdrew her hands.

Her face was not much altered. The eyes were smaller and closer together, with pale stubby lashes. The nose was broader at its base and more upturned, and the mouth thin-lipped and wide. Her chin was round instead of pointed, and her neck gangled in a familiar bow.

But she wasn't *ugly*. Merely somewhat plainer.

"Marielle." Sarah of Netherford moaned. "Our Marielle, what have you done?"

"Mama," said Florelle and Aurielle, stricken as they reached for her.

Marielle flung them off. "Get away from me! Miserable, mewling creatures! Constant reminders of what I most despise, you ugly little toads!"

Her daughters backed away, aghast, as she staggered toward the center of the room. "So what?" she said to her enraptured audience, spreading her arms wide. "So I bargained with a fairy when I was young. It's not a crime. I saw an opportunity and I took it."

"Like you did with Nanette?" Eugenie asked.

"Oh, precious Nanette," Marielle spat. "I gave her a *job*, and all she could do was dote on you. 'Isn't she such a pretty girl?' You were supposed to die of that illness, you little wretch, and she nursed you through the worst of it. Then she caught the influenza in the village and died in her own bed. And who can blame me for switching the pair of you?" Her words lowered into a growl. "Who can blame me now?" She launched herself at Eugenie.

Shrieks erupted from the crowd. Eugenie, stunned, barely had time to raise defensive hands as they toppled to the floor. Marielle grappled at her throat, but the struggle ended almost as soon as it began. Bodies wrenched her back, pinning her by her elbows. A protective arm around Eugenie's waist tucked her away from further danger.

She looked up in wonder at Pip upon the floor beside her.

When had he left his throne?

Marielle thrashed against her restraints, to no avail. Her voice rose in a frenzied pitch. "It's not fair! It's not fair!"

"I think we've heard enough," said the queen, and a hush descended upon that stentorian decree.

Eugenie, self-conscious, extracted herself from Pip's safekeeping and stood, hardly worse for wear. Cautiously she approached her stepmother, considering her. The court held its collective breath as it waited for her to speak.

But Marielle broke the silence instead, hatred oozing from her. "I should've smothered you in your sleep and tossed your body in the pond before we left this morning."

A bolt of fear shot through Eugenie, at how close she had come to an unnatural end. "What stopped you?"

Her stepmother lifted her chin, deigning not to answer.

"Isn't it obvious?" The redheaded fairy, almost forgotten in the fracas, glided between the pair with catlike satisfaction upon her face. "She was afraid."

"Afraid?" Eugenie said.

"Afraid," the creature repeated, and she tapped Marielle's nose to emphasize the word. The woman grimaced. The fairy, meanwhile, twirled around Eugenie as if to music only she could hear. "A counterfeit can't exist without a masterpiece. She thought if she killed you herself, the glamour on her would disappear."

Eugenie's brows drew together, her confusion manifesting as she followed the fairy's flighty movements. "What?"

"It's simple, my child. She is fairy-cursed and you are fairy-blessed. In the same hour that she made her bargain, you were born with everything she desired: beauty, title, fortune, charm—only yours is genuine and hers was fake. There has to be balance." The fairy twirled again, a euphoric giggle on her lips. "When she found you, she knew what you were, but she was afraid—afraid that if she killed you, she would revert to her old ugly self again. So she delayed, hoping to marry her ugly girls into a fortune so their futures and her own would be secure. And once they were settled, she would dispose of you free and clear. It was a lovely plan, and you, so innocent and obedient, would have played right into it. Aren't you lucky to have a godmother like me?"

Her tinkling laugh carried to the high ceiling. Eugenie, stricken, looked to her stepmother for confirmation of this tale.

Marielle's face twisted in contempt. "How is there balance? How can one person have everything, and another have nothing at all?"

Behind her, the younger Elles huddled together and the older couple clung to one another. Sorrow and horror played upon their faces, grief-stricken at the monstrous actions of someone they loved—and who loved them not in return.

"You had far more than you realized," Eugenie said, her own dearth of family never so keen as in this moment. "You cast it aside because you couldn't see its worth."

Her stepmother hissed, lurching as though she would attack again, but her captors held her fast. Even so, Pip hooked Eugenie's elbow and pulled her further back from the seething woman.

"Take her away," said the queen upon her dais. "We will judge what to do with her when we have reviewed the extent of her crimes."

Palace guards escorted Marielle from the room, along with her daughters. Her parents, after a tentative glance toward the throne, followed amid murmurs from the crowd.

"Fernand." The queen locked gazes with her son and pointedly tipped her head toward his vacant chair.

He spared Eugenie an apologetic glance before he left her side again.

"You are, I believe," said the queen to Eugenie, "as yet underage."

A blush crawled up her neck. "Yes," she said, toying nervously with her fingertips. Her twentieth birthday was still half a year away.

Queen Patrice swept a commanding gaze across the gawking throng. "It is with great pleasure that the Crown of Jacondria reinstates the House of Pluterra among its noble families. The Marchioness of Pluterra, Eugenie Vivienne, shall remain under guardianship of the crown until she reaches her majority. Complaints against Baroness Lavande, if there be any, may be registered with the bailiff of the court. You are all dismissed."

Conversations buzzed louder than a beehive. The fairy, beside Eugenie once again, clapped her hands and declared, "That was the best mischief I've seen in decades!" She lighted a kiss upon Eugenie's cheek. Then, in a swirl of sparks, she vanished to nothing but her firefly heart, which winked out of sight.

The queen and her consort stood to vacate the room. Pip bounded from his seat, but he slowed upon the dais steps. Tentatively, he offered Eugenie his hand as token that she should go with them.

Uncertainty gleamed in his eyes.

Why had he so blatantly withheld the truth?

Yet she placed her hand in his, and arm in arm they followed his parents from the hall.

15
Enlightenment

THE DOUBLE DOORS into the antechamber closed, and the queen halted.

"Dominic, go with your father."

Pip opened his mouth, but her tone brooked no argument. Prince Renaud tipped his head, his expression gentle, and proceeded out a second door, never watching whether his son followed. Pip, after pressing Eugenie's hand with a pleading glance, obeyed his mother's decree. He looked back as he crossed into the long hall, and again when he caught up with his father.

How strange and hauntingly familiar, to have someone conscious of her existence once more.

Queen Patrice waited until the father and son were out of sight before she spoke. "He never told you who he was."

"No," said Eugenie, fighting back instinctive hurt on that point. How, with everything that had passed between them, had he not trusted her?

The queen sighed. "My poor boy. This must have been so confusing for you." With softened expression, she reached for Eugenie and guided her through a different exit. "He's 'Prince

Soot and Slipper

Fernand' in public and 'Dominic' in private. We made the distinction when he was quite small, and for his own peace of mind. Theo used to tease him that people only liked him because of his rank."

Theo—Lord Mereloye, as Eugenie now knew—would be a cousin to the prince on his father's side. No wonder the pair had been so familiar with one another.

"I suppose he still clings to that fear in some form," said the queen as they traversed a long marble hall. Her shoes clicked against the floor, while Eugenie's worn slippers made not a sound. "Or perhaps it's because he met you at a masquerade while pretending to be less than he was." She paused in front of a wide door and favored Eugenie with a kindly smile. "Serves him right to have his tricks turned back on him like that."

She motioned Eugenie inside. Sunlight poured through airy curtains upon a lovely sitting room. The queen led her to a couch against the far wall. On a low table, fragrant steam wafted from a silver teapot, with biscuits and cakes piled high on a matching platter. The queen poured a cup and offered it to her guest, who took it with a self-conscious glance around the room.

The things Eugenie had brought from the manor house were propped in an adjacent chair, her childhood family gazing upon the royal tête-à-tête. Her heart squeezed painfully in her chest, its wound still fresh from her stepmother's betrayal. In a way, she was more alone in the world than she ever had been. She averted her eyes and sipped her tea to calm these troubled thoughts.

Queen Patrice resumed their conversation when she had poured her own cup. "He didn't want the royal masquerades to start again. In fact, he vowed he wouldn't attend, and when I commanded it, he arranged his ridiculous plan with Theo."

The mystery of the masquerade prince unfolded on that simple disclosure. "So Theo was the popinjay," said Eugenie in wonder.

The queen tipped her head. "And the goldfish. And, despite his protestations to the contrary, he enjoyed every minute of the spectacle. The boys switched their costumes right before the unmasking, and no one has been the wiser so far."

Theo's enjoyment notwithstanding, the scheme suited Pip to a button. "As a domino, he could go wherever he liked without anyone taking notice," Eugenie said.

"Without having to take notice of anyone in return, too. He wasn't interested in playing nice while lords and ladies jockeyed for position around him. He's always been very intense, that boy, though I suppose you've surmised as much."

Eugenie reflected on the charge. She wouldn't have called him intense, but he was single-minded. "Why didn't he want the masquerades to start again?"

"Because he was broken-hearted, and he didn't want it to mend."

A pang shot through her, uncertainty laced with . . . jealousy, perhaps? So someone had broken the prince's heart, then. No wonder he skulked in the shadows above the dancing throngs. Perhaps the woman who had spurned him moved among them. "I'm sorry to hear that," Eugenie said, feeling instinctively inferior to the phantom coquette.

The queen, teacup poised halfway to her lips, spared her a sidelong glance. "Yes, it was a sorry affair. He'd fallen in love in his youth, but the girl he'd set his heart on died three years ago of the influenza."

Eugenie choked on her drink. She coughed and raised huge eyes to the monarch, who wore a hidden smile.

"Or so we believed. He didn't tell you that, either."

Crimson as a cardinal, she shook her head.

Queen Patrice hummed and took another sip of her tea. "Poor boy. It was at your mother's funeral—most inappropriate, I know, but he was smitten. Starry-eyed and walking on clouds, and when we got home I had to sit him down and explain that you both were too young for him to pursue any lasting attachment and that, as you had just experienced a death in the family, your heart was tender and he needed to take care not to burden or injure it further. He settled for writing you in friendship instead."

The letters of yore—polite, well-worded things—flashed through Eugenie's memory. "I thought he wrote to lots of people."

"No. You were the only one."

This revelation stoked a thread of vanity within her, summoning that child-self who had reveled in each letter despite more practical beliefs that they were written out of courtesy. She squelched the exultant feeling. "He always signed his full name, like it was an official correspondence."

The queen chuckled. "And how much of that do you recall?"

Eugenie rattled off the beginning. "Louis Fernand Renaud Theophilus..."

"...Antonin Dominic Charles," Queen Patrice finished with a fond expression.

Even if she had remembered that mouthful, Eugenie would never have connected "Dominic" to Prince Fernand. The more she learned, the more foolish she felt.

"The letters had to stop when your father remarried, of course," Queen Patrice said.

"Is that why Pip—Dominic—never liked Marielle?"

"Oh no. He disliked her from sheer pettiness. He went to the wedding hoping to talk to you, and she sent you home before he got the chance." She laughed at the memory. "Don't tell him I told you that. He's had a chip on his shoulder ever since and bristles when anyone so much as mentions her." A somber expression replaced her mirth as quickly as it had come. "But he blamed her for your death, too, though he never said as much aloud."

The atmosphere in the room shifted. The queen set her teacup on the table and angled herself to face Eugenie more fully. Conscious of this attention, Eugenie placed her cup down as well. She fought the urge to pull at her fingertips as she so often did when she was nervous.

"We received word of your death the same week he returned home from his study abroad," said the queen. She clasped Eugenie's hands and squeezed. "I've never seen someone so devastated. I hadn't realized how highly he thought of you until that very moment. It had always been a sweet little infatuation before, something we assumed would fade with time, as childhood infatuations often do."

A self-conscious blush blossomed upon the girl's cheeks, and her adoration for Pip redoubled, that he had suffered such grief on her behalf.

"I've watched my boy in silent mourning for the past three years," said Queen Patrice. "Distant, bitter, disconsolate. When his mask came off after that first masquerade, for the first time in years, a spark of happiness lit his eyes, and it kindled hope within my heart. When he admitted his delight had come from the company of a fellow masquerader, doubly so. At that point, I didn't care who you were—peasant or noble, servant or master. You restored my carefree boy to me. I prayed you would return the following week, but of course, everything fell apart that time. He had my blessing to seek you out, to make right whatever had upset you.

"So you can imagine my surprise," she finished, "when he burst into my breakfast room yesterday afternoon and announced that Eugenie of Pluterra was alive, and that Baroness Lavande was the wickedest villain ever to walk the earth."

The image invoked both a sense of awe and the instinct to laugh. Eugenie ducked her head, her overabundance of emotions driving her too close to tears. "Somehow I've caused more trouble than I thought possible, and without the slightest idea I was doing it."

"If you were fairy-blessed at birth, it's no wonder. That explains why your mother was so protective of you, and yet how you ended up with only two names."

Eugenie frowned, a voiceless question in her eyes.

"Fairies always announce to parents when they've chosen a child to watch over," said Queen Patrice knowingly, "usually within an hour or two of the birth, and the parents have no say in the matter. If they give the child too many names, the fairies take it as an insult and curse the child instead. And it's not that your pleasant attributes come from them, but that they appoint themselves as guardians, so to speak, to protect you from harm. It's like having a wild animal adopt you, though I might prefer a bear or a wolf. Fairies being what they are, mischief inevitably follows even their best intentions."

"So 'godmother' really does mean something different to them," Eugenie said.

The queen chuckled. "Quite. If we could outlaw dealings with the creatures, I would, but that would insult them as well. Your fairy godmother seems to have more patience than others I've seen—that she could carry on a bargain with a mortal for almost two decades, for one thing, but that she allowed you to live in seclusion for three years before she interfered as well.

They're capricious creatures, though, so I doubt we'll ever know her true motives."

"She said she wanted to restore balance," said Eugenie. "I didn't really believe her."

"She restored it in the end, so perhaps she spoke the truth."

Was the world back in balance, then? Everything felt uncertain and unfamiliar.

But what had she expected? A restoration to her proper place could not restore the quiet life she had led since her illness. Nor did she want it restored. The fairy had been right: she had been slowly dying in seclusion on that estate.

"What will happen to Marielle?" she asked.

"She deceived and defrauded the crown. Her title is forfeit, and she'll go to prison or exile, whichever better suits her crimes."

"And the younger Elles?"

The queen's eyes crinkled at the nickname, though she sobered almost as quickly. She spoke with care, weighing her words. "It all depends. They were complicit with their mother's deceit, but to what degree filial loyalty played a part—whether they approved or whether she coerced them—will largely determine their fate. If possible, I would like to give them into the care of their grandparents, two girls in recompense for the two they have lost, along with a healthy stipend and the crown's deepest condolences. I would not have wished today's revelations on any feeling parent."

Eugenie shivered against her memory of sweet, well-meaning Nanette, whose bones lay cold in a borrowed grave. The maid had been only a year or two older than her, kind and cheerful. She deserved a better end than the one she had received—particularly her own sister using her as cover for a greater crime. Marielle might have murdered Eugenie any time these past three years had her vanity not kept her from the deed, and no one would have been the wiser.

"And what's going to become of me?" The words left her lips on little more than a whisper. How small and selfish, that she could even wonder; her fortunes had been reversed, while others' would be damaged from this day forward.

Queen Patrice seemed to think no less of her for the question, though. She patted Eugenie's clasped hands, compassion softening her regal face. "Your future is largely yours to determine. I will say this, however: you hold my son's heart in your power. Whatever your own feelings may be—and he knows not to press you in this time of crisis—please deal with him kindly."

In wonder Eugenie met the monarch's gaze. Silently she nodded, robbed of any other response.

16
Dreams Rekindled

A LONG, HOT BATH ebbed away the stress of the afternoon, of the past few days. The queen gave Eugenie rooms of her own as a ward of the crown. Accustomed to tending to herself, she submitted in bewilderment to the ministrations of three busy maids who helped her dress and brushed her hair until it gleamed. The girls, younger than her by a few years, treated her like a porcelain doll that might break if handled too roughly.

They never spoke directly to her, and Eugenie, overwhelmed, could think of nothing to say to them except her gratitude.

When they left, she stared at her pristine reflection in the full-length mirror.

Her old, worn clothing had had the comfort of familiarity, and the fairy's costumes had been like something out of a dream. The dress she wore now, a sedate blue that made her eyes bright, had fabric as fine as anything Marielle wore, with meticulous tailoring and delightful embroidery along its sleeves and hemline. It was nothing opulent, but she felt like a different creature wearing it, a butterfly that had emerged from its drab chrysalis.

She had never belonged among the Elles, even when her father was alive. She knew now that, for all their posturing to the contrary, they had never wanted her to belong.

But could she belong with the prince?

The queen expected her to join the royal family for dinner, though she almost would have preferred to eat by herself. Her nerves whirled like a windstorm. Rather than wait for a summons, she determined to walk off some of the erratic energy. She took a deep breath and opened her bedroom door.

Pip stood on the other side, one hand poised to knock. On a sharp inhale, he stepped backward, hiding his hand behind him like a child caught in mischief.

Eugenie's heart leapt against her ribcage. She stepped into the hall and pulled the door shut behind her, then leaned against it.

"Why didn't you tell me you were the prince?"

He flinched, shame flashing across him. "I should have, but . . ." After a fleeting glance, he looked away to the wall. "You didn't recognize me."

Was he *sulking*?

Her pulse quickened all the more. She ducked to catch his attention. "Should I have? You stood right next to me while the prince pranced among his guests."

"That was—"

"Theo? I know. But you didn't know who I was either until I as much as told you."

"That's because you were—"

"Supposed to be dead. I know." She allowed herself a wan smile as she leaned against the door again, still holding to the knob behind her for support.

He fixed a steady, contrite gaze upon her. She could have drowned in his eyes and died happy.

"I'm sorry. I should have told you. I didn't want to complicate things any more than they already were, or to scare you off, and I didn't want you to act toward me out of duty, either. I could be close to you as the anonymous Pip, a confidant and a help. I didn't think Prince Fernand would have the same liberties."

A smile threatened to manifest, but she kept it under tight control. "You thought I was so inconstant?"

"No. Just—before I knew it, the truth was too awkward to tell. At the end, I even worried I couldn't live up to your image of my younger self."

She snorted a laugh and quickly covered her mouth.

"You think that's funny?" Pip asked in wonder.

She nodded, not trusting herself to speak.

At last he recognized the tease behind her line of questions. His expression turned grave. "You know my heart, Eugenie of Pluterra. I can only guess half of what my mother told you, and I'm forbidden from any attempts to engage your sensibilities until the dust of this calamity settles. But in the meantime, will you forgive me, or will you leave me in agony?"

The queen was right. He was intense, but in the very best way.

His reasoning was also sound. Had he told her he was the prince, she would have distanced herself on instinct, embarrassed and convinced that she shouldn't burden someone of such lofty rank.

But that hardly mattered anymore.

Eugenie matched his fervency with her own. "You are forgiven. And you know perfectly well that my sensibilities were already engaged."

In relief, he swept her into his arms. She shut her eyes, her knotted anxiety dissipating. For fully a minute they stood in silent contentment, each drawing comfort from the other's embrace.

Soot and Slipper

"You do know that when you brought your other shoe today you staked a public claim on my heart," said Pip. "That means you have to marry me."

She huffed a laugh and swatted his shoulder. "Is that really how you're going to ask?"

He drew back, his eyes alight with mirth. "Will you—?"

"Of course I will," she said before he could finish, and she kissed him with all her soul.

The End

About the Author

KATE STRADLING was among the bayous born
But soon thereafter moved to other lands
Where sun and wind kept vistas sere and worn
And cactus thrived amid the desert sands.
Though blessed with countless relatives and kin,
In quiet reading was her soul most fed.
When books no longer filled the void within,
She took to making stories in her head.
Some say that's where she probably went wrong.
The stories now consume her waking hours.
Her love of language waxes ever strong,
And all her other interests devours.
In prose she babbles, but it could be worse.
At least she isn't writing things in verse.

Printed in Great Britain
by Amazon